MAYHEM ON THE MIND

KARI LEE TOWNSEND

OLIVERHEBERBOOKS

This book is dedicated to all the people who rescue fur babies in need and adopt purebreds. They all need good homes and people to love them. I personally can't imagine my life without my two Samoyeds, Cozmo (7) and Caya (5). They have the same father, Zeppelin, but different mothers, Chara and Peach, and about the sweetest dispositions you can imagine.
The next series is yours, kids!

1

"Home sweet home, Ballas." Detective Nikos Stevens walked between his half of the house and mine, wearing basketball shorts and a muscle shirt while sipping his morning coffee. Notes of mocha and earthy aftershave wafted to my nose.

No matter what the man was doing, he always smelled so good.

Spring in Clearview Connecticut was still pretty chilly, but my half-Greek half-Viking detective was a walking furnace and dressed accordingly. He had the tall, dark good looks of a Greek god and the muscular body of an ancient Viking, never failing to make me weak in the knees.

I shook the distracting thoughts from my mind and frowned. "*Is* our home sweet, Detective?" I winced, swiping dust particles away from my face three times then covering my cup of steaming hot tea with its steeping lid.

He shrugged. "A little dust never hurt anyone."

"I'll have you know that fine dust particles can penetrate deep into the lungs and contribute to respiratory problems." I waved my hand around, gesturing to the mess. "I'm not sure all *this* was such a good idea."

He wagged his finger in front of my face. "Oh, no you don't. You're not getting out of moving in with me that easily." He pointed to the big gaping hole where a solid wall used to divide our apartments. "If I remember correctly, *you're* the one who put the first hole there with a sledgehammer not that long ago. It would have been fixed by now, but someone couldn't make up her mind about how to move forward."

"Putting a hole in the wall was a brief moment of insanity," I mumbled, but there was no going back now.

He pulled me into his arms and kissed me. *I'm crazy about you, too, babe.* He was the only man to ever get me out of my own head and make me stop overthinking everything. With a wink, he let go of me and inspected the progress of the remodel.

Ever since I'd fallen from the loft where I design my Kalli Original lingerie in my best friend, Jaz's, clothing store, I'd woken up with the gift of reading minds. But I could only hear a person's thoughts when touching them.

A nightmare for a germaphobe like me.

The only people who knew about my ability were Jaz and Nik—other than the lovely couple, Sunny and Mitch Stone, we met on our cruise to Bermuda and the captain of the ship, but that's another story. I didn't mind Sunny knowing because she had a secret of her own. She was psychic, and her husband happened to be a detective as well.

The four of us hit it off right from the start.

Nik and I had just returned from our vacation, if you could call surviving the Devil's Triangle then being on lockdown in the middle of the Atlantic

Ocean and solving a murder investigation a vacation. Even with an ocean between us, Ma and Aunt Tasoula had still managed to get into loads of trouble. But Nik and I were back in Clearview Connecticut, and life had returned to normal.

Well, however normal it could be with our big, fat, Greek families.

Frankly, I was just glad all the drama was over. It was spring. A time for new beginnings. Time to take our relationship to the next level and move in together. I frowned as old doubts crept in. I was worried moving in together would be the end of our relationship. I liked peace, quiet, and order in my life, while Nik's life was chaos with a capital C.

Nik had a big sloppy Saint Bernard named Wolfgang, and I had a prissy calico cat named Priscilla. They weren't exactly a match made in heaven. As for me, I was extremely clean and orderly, while my boyfriend had three sides to him. Detective Stevens was all about following protocol. Nik the nice guy would try his best. While Nikos the Greek would be messy just to get a rise out of me.

What had I been thinking?

"I don't have to read minds to know what you're thinking," he said softly as he walked past me, and I jumped. "It's all going to work out, Ballas. You'll see." He winked and touched my cheek, then kept moving.

The house was a huge colonial on Picture Perfect Drive off Main Street. Jaz still owned the house. I had lived with her in one half of the house, and she had rented the other half to Nik. After she moved in with her fiancé, Detective Boomer Matheson, I took over the rest of the mortgage payment for our half of the house.

For now, Nik and I still lived in our own parts of

the house. The pets roamed free between the two apartments while the remodel was being finished. We were hoping that would help them get used to each other. All it had done so far was to elevate the level of noise as the chase was constantly on.

Nik had disappeared to get ready to head into the station, while I ventured into my bedroom to get ready to go to work at Full Disclosure. My spring line was already out, but now I needed to come up with new designs for my summer line. Mr. Erickson, my boss at Interludes in NYC, was already pressuring me for a date to turn in my collection.

It was hard to be creative in the middle of chaos.

Not long after, I headed back into the kitchen. Prissy rounded the corner, hissed at me as she ran by, then launched herself up her tree until she scrambled on top of the living room curtain rod. Wolfgang barked and gave chase, skidding to a halt when he saw me.

We had an understanding.

"Don't even think about touching my curtains with that slobbery mouth of yours, Wolfy." I crossed my arms and tapped my foot, shuddering over the thought of how many germs were in his saliva.

He whined, staring up at my cat with adoration shining in his big brown eyes, but he kept his quivering behind on the floor.

I patted him on the top of his massive head three times. "Good boy." Then I thoroughly cleaned my hands with hand sanitizer, of course.

Nik joined me in the kitchen and moments later, his cell rang.

"Stevens here." He stopped walking and his eyes grew wide.

That couldn't be a good sign.

"That many?" he asked...more like croaked.

That *definitely* wasn't a good sign.

Nik frowned. "Well, don't snap at me, Matheson. It takes two to tango, or in this case three. This is just as much their fault as it is his."

I suddenly had a feeling I knew exactly what he was talking about.

"Who said I wouldn't help? I'm not a deadbeat anything. Of course, I'll do the right thing." Nik hung up with a grunt and flushed cheeks.

"What was that about?" I asked, afraid to hear the answer.

"101 Saint Berdoodles," he said with a sigh and a disapproving expression as he glared at Wolfgang.

I gasped, my gaze shooting to the massive Saint Bernard sprawled out on the floor. He yawned, not looking guilty in the least. I crossed my arms and shook my head at the naughty boy, and then blinked.

If I didn't know better, I would swear he was smiling.

~

"Twenty-two puppies, Kalli. Twenty-two!" Jazlyn Alverez flipped her long, thick honey brown curls over her shoulder the second I walked through the front door of Full Disclosure. "What am I supposed to do about that?" She stared me down with amber eyes. She had the gorgeous good looks of her model mother, the genius brain of her banker father, and a warrior spirit.

She'd been my best friend since we were little, and I adored her.

I handed her an extra-large latte and a bag of special pastries that Maria Danza, owner of Sinfully Delicious, had prepared for her. The bakery was right across the street from Full Disclosure. In exchange for the special pastries, Jaz gave Maria a big discount on the clothes in her boutique.

Maria was once Jaz's arch nemesis because of a love triangle they used to be in with a construction worker named Johnny. But now that Jaz was engaged to Boomer and Maria was engaged to Sully Anderson, our parcel delivery person, they were suddenly BFFs. I couldn't be jealous of their friendship because Maria was a sweetheart, and I liked her too.

I sipped my organic tea and tried not to roll my eyes at my friend's dramatics over becoming the lucky owner of twenty-two fur babies. Taking a bite of my healthy organic breakfast bar, I pondered over the right words to say. Somehow *better you than me* didn't sound quite right.

"Congratulations?" I offered with a tentative smile.

"Thank you." Her eyes locked onto mine as she took a sip of her coffee and a bite of one of her treats before replying, "Congratulations to you as well, *Granny*."

I choked on my bar. "Excuse me?"

"Chanel and Versace only contributed to *half* of these babies. Your boy, Wolfy, did the rest. The way I figure it, you and Nik own half of these puppies. Eleven big bundles of joy, with an emphasis on the word *big*." She scowled.

Puppies? My hand jerked and I sloshed my tea. "B-But Wolfgang is Nik's dog." This couldn't be happening. Panic rendered me paralyzed, and I gagged as I imagined Wolfgang's drool times eleven.

Jaz handed me a napkin. "And now that beast is *yours* by association."

"B-But we're not married." I had to force my hand to move so I could wipe up the dribble of tea.

"A minor technicality." Jaz waved her coffee cup around as she talked. "Boomer and I aren't married yet, either."

"At least you're engaged." I tried to reason with her.

"Nice try." She smirked. "You're moving in together; therefore, the puppies will be under both your roofs. Hence, co-parenting."

"Slow down a minute." I took a few deep breaths to calm my racing heart before the thundering beats cracked my chest cavity and tried to think clearly. I didn't know the first thing about raising puppies. There had to be a way out of this crazy situation. "Don't they have to stay with their mothers until they are eight weeks old?"

"Yes, but after that, however many are left that don't get adopted—" she thrust her perfectly manicured fingernail in my direction "—*you're* taking half of them."

I was already shaking my head, feeling my stomach clench into knots. "I don't know if I can handle more than one Wolfgang."

"Neither can I." Jaz huffed out a breath, and for the first time, I could see she was as panicked as I was. "At least you guys have a house," she went on. "We're still living in Boomer's bachelor pad apartment. The twins went into labor on the same day, just hours apart. Scared the heck out of me and Boomer." Chanel and Versace were gorgeous, purebred, full-sized black poodles.

My heart filled with empathy as I put myself in her shoes. "I would have panicked for sure. What did you do?"

"We took them to the vet to give birth, but now

they're back home." She looked at me with real fear in her eyes, voicing my own thoughts. "What am I going to do, Kalli? I don't know the first thing about raising puppies."

"You're not alone, Jaz." My gaze softened. "We'll get through this together like we do everything else."

She inhaled a shaky breath and nodded her thanks. "When we rescued the poodles, they were fully grown. Boomer's home with the puppies because they can't be left alone this young. The vet gave us information on puppy whelping. Boomer's confident we'll make great puppy parents. I'm not so sure. Let's just say I've never been so happy to go to work."

"Same here. Nik was on his way over to help out after Boomer called this morning. He sounded a little frazzled. Nik has had Wolfgang since he was a puppy, but that was years ago. I'm sure he's a little rusty, and I don't know anything about raising puppies, either. Prissy's a cat." I took a calming breath, held it, then released it as I tried to look at the bright side of the situation. "At least they're half poodle. Let's both pray they take after their mamas."

"Amen to that."

Full Disclosure was a clothing boutique in the business district. It was a quaint store with fabulous clothes for all occasions. She had a burgundy microfiber sofa in the sitting area next to the dressing rooms. Decorative pin-striped pillows were placed strategically on the sofa with a matching love seat that sat kitty corner to that.

I rented the loft upstairs. I could look down on the store below, but no one was allowed to come up unless I said so. It was my own personal space to create my designs. I had a large mirror, various types of fabric, pins of all sizes, and a mannequin to drape my designs over, with hand sanitizer at the top of the stairs, of course. The buzz of shoppers down below had always inspired me. That was why I rented the space from her. To keep my finger on the pulse of what women of all shapes, sizes, and ages wanted.

It was early. The store wasn't open just yet. Jaz's employees filed in one at a time, waved to us, then started getting things ready to open. Victoria Nettles, the new town handywoman, came out of the storage room. "The leak's all set, Ms. Alvarez."

"Please, call me Jaz."

The petite dynamo with a strawberry blond ponytail and a toolbelt smiled wide. "Only if you call me Vicky."

"Well, thank you, Vicky. I appreciate it." Jaz handed the woman a check, and she saluted us on her way out.

We took what was left of our goodies and sat on the couch with our morning beverages. "How's the wedding planning going?" I changed the subject and moved over to the comfy furniture.

Jaz sighed, looking exhausted. "I am so tired. I don't know which way is up. I was making good progress before the babies came."

"You still want that barn for your reception?" I sipped my tea.

"I think so. I just hope we won't have to postpone the wedding." She frowned then took another bite of her pastry.

"You won't. It's only spring. There is still plenty of time. The puppies should all be adopted by summer."

"*Should* being the operative word." Jaz tucked a strand of hair behind her ear.

Jaz looked like a goddess. Meanwhile, Boomer had unruly russet colored hair, hazel eyes, and a long, lean body. He wore jeans and his leather bomber jacket with a different t-shirt most days, whereas Jaz dressed in designer clothes on the daily. No one thought they would last, but all you had to do was see them together to know they were crazy about each other.

Meanwhile, I was all solid color suits with my long, golden-blond hair pulled into my standard chignon. Prim and proper was what I called it. Uptight and starched was what Ma called it. Nik was all jeans, button-down shirts, and sport coats, when he wasn't in his shorts, that is. He wore them year-round when he was off duty.

We were about as opposite as they came, yet we'd lasted longer than most had predicted as well. Opposites attracted, that was why glamourous Jaz and boring me had been inseparable since we were little. I was adopted by a big, fat Greek family, and she was the gorgeous flower that had never quite fit in.

We got each other.

Now that she had settled down and was engaged to Boomer, all the eligible bachelors in town had stopped chasing her. That went a long way towards endearing her to more of the women in Clearview.

The bells over the front door chimed and in walked Ma and Aunt Tasoula. Ma patted her big poof of teased black beehive hair then smoothed her peach polyester pantsuit. Meanwhile, Aunt Tasoula wore her dark hair a little too long and her clothes a lot too tight. They spotted us and scurried over, their hands moving nonstop along with their lips.

"Where are they?" Ma clapped her hands and stared at Jaz with big brown eyes.

"Where are who?" Jaz studied Ma with a puckered brow.

"My grandbabies." She patted her large bosom.

I spit out my tea. "Ma, they're puppies. *Not* grandbabies."

She shrugged. "You no give me babies. They all I get."

I mentally slapped my forehead. "You adopted Jasper, so now you have twice the chance for real grandbabies."

She grunted but then her whole face softened. "He good boy."

Boy? Jasper was a full-grown man. He was my half-brother on my biological mother's side. We had just found each other, and he had been welcomed by my entire family with open arms. It didn't matter that he was an adult, Ma insisted on making him hers. Jasper had never had anyone want him, so he was all too happy to play along. My parents adopted him and had Father Papadopoulos baptize him.

Now, apparently, he was Greek, too.

"How's your 40th high school reunion planning going?" Jaz asked Aunt Tasoula and shot me a conspiratorial wink.

Aunt Tasoula launched into a rant.

Ma rolled her eyes.

And I breathed a sigh of relief the attention was off grand-anything.

"She better no try to steal my man," Aunt Tasoula's angry words snapped me back to attention.

"Who?" I asked.

"Skylar Delaney. Her arch nemesis," Ma said dramatically.

"That Medusa wannabe tried to steal my sweet drummer boy, Leon, back in high school, Zeus rest his soul." Aunt Tasoula and Ma both made the sign of the cross before my aunt continued. "Just because she head cheerleader no mean she better than me. I twirl my baton better than she twirl her body. Skylar The Flyer? She no fly. They just throw her around." Aunt Tasoula sniffed sharply and then studied her fingernails with a smug look on her face. "I have better pompoms anyway."

Ma grunted.

Aunt Tasoula's smug look twisted into a scowl. "If she try to steal my Tate, I set her hair on fire. I do that once, you know. My flaming baton burn toupee off Principal Wimble's head. Burn bald spot bad. It's true. I try to make new hair from my dog clippings, but he no happy with me."

"What you expect, 'Soula? Rigby's fur orange, black, and white." Ma threw her hands up.

Aunt Tasoula shrugged. "Oh, well." She winked. "That when I know I want to be a cosmopolitan."

"Cosmetologist, you nitwit. Now focus," Ma snapped. "You no have man for Skylar to steal, remember? You and Tate on break."

"Break, shmake." My aunt brushed her long hair over her shoulder. "I decide I take him back."

"Does he know that?" Ma raised a brow.

"No, but he will. He better no give me hard time. No one touch my big, blond Viking but me."

The bells over the shop chimed and in walked a stunning older woman.

"Speak of the devil," Ma muttered.

"And she is most definitely wearing Prada," Jaz added, giving her the once over.

"So much for no more drama." I sighed.

Skylar and my aunt locked eyes. We didn't need a flaming baton for sparks to fly between them, and someone was most definitely going to get burned.

It was going to be one long week.

2

The Greeks have a tradition called the Red and White Marti Bracelet. The bracelet is made out of red and white thread. Red symbolizes strength, protection, passion, and life. While white represents purity and the coming of spring. The bracelet is worn during the month of March to protect against spring diseases. Then at the first sign of spring, it is tied to a flowering tree.

I hadn't worn one on my cruise, sending Ma and Aunt Tasoula into a fit of the vapors with worry over me sailing into the Bermuda Triangle unprotected. Now that March was over, they had convinced the family to tie their bracelets around trees at Aphrodite's restaurant and Hera's Halo salon so they would both have good luck.

Once again, I was to blame since I hadn't worn the bracelet or tied it around the tree out front of Full Disclosure. Therefore, Skylar showing up in town early and wreaking all kinds of havoc this past week was my doing, of course. Sunday brunch, after mass at our Greek Orthodox church with Father Papadopoulos, at my parents' place was one place where Skylar couldn't go.

So that's where we all were.

Spring was warming up quickly in Clearview, Connecticut. My family held brunch outside as often as they could. They had a two-story colonial with a big backyard. A large gazebo strung with lights was stocked with overflowing food tables, and the yard was filled with picnic tables, marble statues, and a fountain surrounded by plants that were already beginning to flower. The air was fresh and new.

What else could possibly go wrong?

The Ballas and Pagonis families practically made up half the town, with the mamas taking turns hosting Sunday brunch. They all get along really well, but the Greeks are passionate people. And competitive. They constantly try to outdo each other on every occasion. Their neighbors had given up on trying to stop the loud music, singing, dancing, "Opa!" shouting, Ouzo drinking Sunday shenanigans.

"I'm exhausted." Jaz joined my side with a full plate. Boomer and Nik were still filling theirs at the buffet.

Jaz and Boomer weren't Greek and didn't go to our church, but every Sunday they were invited to join us for brunch. The mamas were obsessed with anyone who was in love. The same went for my biological father, Father Michael Connery, who was a Catholic priest. After we had finally found each other, he had stayed in town to get to know me and had become good friends with our Greek church's priest, Father Angelino Papadopoulos.

"Kalli, are you listening to me." Jaz huffed out a breath.

I winced, tossing my half-eaten gyro into the trash. "I'm sorry. I can't imagine how rough whelping twenty-two puppies must be." Babies of any kind terrified me because I still wasn't sure if I wanted children or not, and I needed to figure that out before even contemplating marriage. Not that Nik had proposed, but he might someday. That was part of the reason why I was dragging my feet in finishing the remodel.

The minute we knocked out that wall for good, there would be no turning back.

"Milly has been a godsend. She stops by every day to dog sit if Boomer and I have to go to work and Nik or you can't take a turn." Jaz shook her head. "I don't know what I'm going to do if she gives birth before the puppies are adopted."

Milly Donovan was a dog walker and she worked at Dino Willis's doggy daycare. That was how both Jaz and Nik had met her. Now she was married to jewelry store owner, Nelson Rockwell, and was in her last trimester for their first child.

"That was smart putting the furniture from the guest bedroom in storage and a baby gate on the door. It makes the perfect puppy room."

"We had to do something." Nik's cousin Thalia was a real estate agent and looking for the perfect home for them, when she wasn't dating her new boyfriend, Senator Parker West. "Lucky for us," Jaz continued, "our landlord has been very accommodating, mostly because she wants to adopt one of the puppies when they're old enough. Apparently, these mixed doodle breeds are all the rage with their mixed white, brown, and black curly shaggy coat."

"I'm not a dog person, but even I can admit Saint Berdoodles are adorable." Especially the runt of this litter. She is a sweetheart.

"These dogs are known for their friendly and gentle nature. According to my research, they are good-natured, social, affectionate, and great with children. Poodles are highly intelligent, and Saint Berdoodles inherit that trait, thank Zeus. That means they'll be obedient and easy to train, which should help when finding them homes. And they make great watchdogs, as they inherit the protective instincts of a Saint Bernard. I can attest to that. Wolf is very loyal and protective of his family."

I studied her curiously. "What was with the paint on their tails, though?"

Jaz shrugged. "Milly is a dog whisperer with an encyclopedia of facts for a brain when it comes to most breeds. She told us everything we needed to do to take care of these puppies. It was her idea to use a dog safe spray paint to paint the tip of each puppy's tail with a different color shade so we could tell them all apart. The girls are all bold shades like their strong, confident mamas, while the boys are all pastels since Wolfgang is one big marshmallow."

"That's ingenious. I never would have thought to do that." I felt guilty over Wolf's part in all this. "I wish we could help out more, but I wouldn't trust Wolf not to squish one by accident or Prissy not to scratch them."

"You and Nik both taking turns dog sitting is more help than you know." Jaz squeezed my arm. *But I have to say it's cured my baby fever.*

I laughed and gave her a wink that clearly said, *I'm right there with you, sister.*

Talk of babies made me think of spring fever and Greek mamas on a mission. It was like something came over them, turning them into matchmaking monsters. It was a scary time of year for all the single men and women around Clearview. My cousins Silas and Kosmos ran a diner. They were already paired up with bartender Zena and mail carrier Winnie. My other cousin Yanni ran a landscaping business. He was now dating his assistant Claudett. While Nik's cousin Thalia was paired up with the senator.

My gaze settled on my cousin Eleni.

She had long gorgeous dark hair and a killer smile, but for some reason, she had the worst luck when it came to dating. She worked in my parents' restaurant as a waitress, and her sister Frona washed dishes in the back. Frona had fallen off the apple cart when she was young and had never been the same, but she was happy and fun and a handful for my YiaYia, who looked out for her every day.

Frona bounced by on her pogo stick, naming off all the puppies with each bounce as her lopsided pigtails swung wildly in the breeze and the pompom stuffed in her back pocket shook to the beat. Aunt Tasoula cursed, Leni scolded, and YiaYia gave chase, her black scarf tied around her gray bun flowing behind her in a blaze of matriarch glory.

Leni was the only one currently single, other than my new Greek brother, Jasper. My pop and papou were deep in conversation with him at this very moment, while the mamas brought more food out with their eagle eyes trained on them.

Nik and Boomer wove their way through the craziness to join us.

"I can only guess what Pop is saying to Jasper." I groaned.

"We need to find you a nice Greek girl," Nik replied with the perfect accent and amount of rasp in the back of his throat. "With your papou adding, *You go make Greek babies. Okay? Okay. It's settled.*"

"There you have it," I added with the same raspy accent, and we all laughed.

Nik's ma, Chloe, was talking to Boomer and Nik's

captain, Quincy Crenshaw. Chloe was a striking woman, all sophistication and class. She'd stolen Quincy's heart as soon as she had moved to Clearview. He was just as striking. Tall, dark, and handsome with salt and pepper hair and steel-gray eyes. It had been awkward for Nik at first, but even he couldn't deny they were meant to be together.

The captain's phone rang, and he frowned. He stepped away from her to answer the call. After a moment, he whispered something into her ear and kissed her cheek. Turning, he scanned the crowd until he spotted Nik and Boomer, before making a beeline for us with long, purposeful strides.

"Well, that can't be good." Boomer sighed, shoving the last of his roasted eggplant Moussaka with lamb in his mouth.

"I was thinking the same thing." Nik groaned before popping the last bite of his Spanakopita spinach pie with its flaky crust into his mouth and moaning in pleasure as he looked up to the sky as if thanking the gods for their masterpiece creation.

Captain Crenshaw came to a stop by the four of us with a serious expression on his face. "Ladies." Always the gentleman, he tipped his head to Jaz and me.

We smiled and waved back.

"What's up, Cap?" Boomer wiped his hands on a napkin.

"Stallone's Supermarket just found a counterfeit bill." The captain looked from Boomer to Nik. "That's the fourth business to get hit this week."

Nik rubbed his whiskered jaw as he drew his eyebrows together in speculation. "Between the spring festival and the 40th class reunion, there are a lot of people in town. It could have come from anywhere."

"Correct." The captain scanned the backyard

packed with our friends and families. "That's why I want to be very thorough in getting to the bottom of this before it spirals out of control, starting now."

"Roger that, Cap." Boomer kissed Jaz's cheek. "Sorry to have to bug out, babe. I'll be back as soon as I can."

"I know you will." Jaz wrapped her arms around her detective and gave him a hug. "I'll head home and relieve Milly. Be careful. You haven't had much sleep."

"Always." He tweaked her nose.

"We're on it, Sir." Nik nodded once to the captain, then turned to me with a puppy dog expression.

"Go on with you then, Detective." I sighed dramatically, but he knew I was teasing. Being called away to investigate a crime went along with dating a detective. That didn't mean I couldn't be a little disappointed.

He kissed my cheek. *I'll make it up to you later, Ballas.* Then he winked and left with Boomer.

"Why do I feel like there's more going on than new beginnings and fresh starts this spring?" Jaz asked.

"Oh, there's trouble in the air for sure. I can smell it. Something tells me there's a whole lot of new drama that's about to happen, and I don't like it."

BY THE TIME I finished tending to our pets and Nik finished questioning the businesses affected by the counterfeit money, it was getting late, and I hadn't planned ahead. We decided to have dinner out somewhere. Except, I only ate at places where I knew the kitchen was immaculate and would allow me to bring my own utensils. Germs freaked me out, but Nik never made me feel like I was weird.

Just one more thing I loved about the man.

We often went to Rosalita's Mexican restaurant. I went to high school with her and knew she was a clean freak. Not to mention, her restaurant was located on the outskirts of town, which gave us at least some privacy.

With both of our families making up a big portion of the town, it was difficult to escape them, but we were both starving. So, we headed to Aphrodite's. Ma always kept a sanitized table and dishes set aside just for me. Same with Aunt Tasoula. She kept a special cape and chair just for me at her hair salon. My family might drive me crazy, but I was sure I did them as well, and family was family.

We all loved each other.

Just like my parents' house and yard, Greek décor with an extra touch of the spring Martis filled the restaurant, giving off the appearance of stepping back in time to ancient Greece. Delicious aromas of traditional Greek food wafted through the air. The dining room was packed with spring festival seekers and high school reunion attendees.

As soon as we walked through the front door, I wished we hadn't.

"Oh, my Zeus, this is not going to end well." I looked up at Nik.

He frowned. "What isn't going to end well?"

So much for the Martis bracelet tied to the tree out front bringing good luck. I pointed over to the far corner of the restaurant. Tate Hemsworth wore a goofy lopsided grin on his chiseled Viking face, while Skylar Delaney stared up at him with a sultry smile as she twirled her bottle blond curls.

A gust of wind blew into the restaurant as the front door swung open.

Aunt Tasoula marched inside wearing white

leather pants, red high heels, and a tight red silk blouse in honor of the red and white Martis colors. Her black hair was teased high at the top and flowing long at the bottom. She must have added extensions for the reunion. Her eyes scanned the restaurant then came to a sizzling stop.

"Skylar Delaney, get you pompoms away from my man!" My aunt thrust her long ruby red fingernail in Tate's direction.

He frowned. "Now, hold on a minute, Tasoula. You made it very clear we were on a break not too long ago."

"I change my mind. No more break." She nodded once, swiping her hand through the air then crossing her arms.

"Well, maybe I haven't changed mine." He arched a thick blond brow at her. "You have no say in how I spend my time these days."

Skylar sat back and folded her hands, resting them in her lap. She wore a slinky black cocktail dress, and a burgundy smirk.

My aunt's face registered shock, then formed a scowl. "She no like you. She just want to make me mad. She married."

"Actually, she's—" Tate started to say to Aunt Tasoula.

"Widowed," Skylar corrected. "You, of all people, should know how that feels." She glared at my aunt.

"Easy, there—" Tate started to warn Skylar.

"I do know how that feels." My aunt patted her chest. "*I* no move on for years. *You* a floozy."

"Hey, now, that's not—" Tate interjected once more, only to be cut off by the women yet again.

"I am no such thing." Skylar's smirk disappeared

into a burgundy pout. "You've always been jealous of me because I was head cheerleader."

"Well, I don't know about—" Tate started to reason.

"Jealous? Ha!" My aunt spun in a perfect pirouette on her toes, throwing her hand in the air in dramatic fashion. "I twirl circles around you with my baton. *You* jealous of *me*. You always want what I have. Even now."

Tate sighed, remaining silent as he looked between the two of them with a tired, helpless expression on his rugged face.

"Like the man said...he's not yours." Skylar preened.

"Ladies!" Tate finally got a word in with a loud, booming voice.

Both women were startled into silence.

"I'm not either of yours," Tate continued with a more calm but firm tone, "and I won't ever be if you both keep acting like children."

"I no child." Aunt Tasoula stood a little straighter and thrust her nose in the air. "But maybe I too much woman for you."

"Sorry, Tate. You're not my only suitor, and this is all a bit too much for any sane person." Sklyar stood and pointed to my aunt. "Your *ex* is crazy." Then she headed over to a table with two men who had to be brothers because they looked just alike. She sat down and fell into conversation with them as if that whole scene hadn't just happened.

"I show you crazy. I gonna make you regret you words." A shriek slipped out of my aunt's mouth, and she lunged after Skylar.

Skylar's eyes bulged and she screamed, cowering behind the brothers.

Tate surged to his feet in one fluid movement and caught Aunt Tasoula around the waist, before she could do something she would regret in front of half her graduating class. All eyes were on her.

My aunt looked around the room as if just now realizing she had an audience. She cleared her throat. "You let me go. I fine now. Remove you tree branch from my waist. Okay? Okay." She patted his massive forearm until he released her. "What's that?" she asked loudly even though I didn't hear anyone speak. "Ophelia need me in kitchen. I go now." Holding her head high, she marched past Skylar without another word...

But something told me the feud between them was far from over.

3

A week had gone by, and the end of the infamous 40th high-school reunion for my aunt's graduating class was upon us, thank the gods. I honestly didn't know how much more Nik and Boomer could take. They had their hands full investigating the counterfeit bills that continued to pop up around town, so getting called away to deal with my aunt and her arch nemesis's shenanigans wasn't helping.

Aunt Tasoula was on the planning committee with other people from her graduating class, but she had pretty much taken over since she still lived in town. And of course, she'd gone over the top on just about everything.

A one-day party had turned into an entire week's worth of events.

I had a standing appointment every six weeks to get my hair trimmed at my aunt's salon, Hera's Halo, inspired by the queen of the gods. I walked through the front door of the Greek themed full-service salon, and it was packed. All the chairs were gold thrones with capes like a queen's robe. The dryers were painted like crowns with precious gems adorning them. There was a swing in one corner and a stripper pole in the other.

My aunt was all about fun, and figured her clients could play while they waited.

I personally gave her *toys* a wide birth, shuddering over the thought of the germs that might be clinging to them. Ma waved me over to a seat she was saving for me. I wiped off the seat with a sanitized wipe and sat down to wait my turn while my aunt finished putting lowlights in my cousin Leni's hair.

The man next to me with blond hair in definite need of a trim glanced at the sanitized wipe in my hand with an expression that gave nothing away, but I could guess what he must be thinking. His green eyes met mine behind small round spectacles and he smiled pleasantly, flashing a set of deep dimples.

I smiled in return before he raised his newspaper and went back to reading. I could appreciate someone else who was old school and still liked to hold a paper in his hands. There were so many new people in town, it was hard to keep up.

"So, how are my grandbabies?" Ma asked, snapping my attention back to her.

I didn't even try to fight it anymore. "Getting big. I can't believe how much they've grown in just a couple of weeks. Milly showed Jaz how to litter box train them. They're so smart, like their mamas, but they're going to be huge like their papa, except maybe the runt of the litter. She's a sweet little thing, with droopy eyes like weeping willow branches when she looks at you. The rest are tanks." The bigger the dog, the more drool it created. I felt my face pale over the thought.

"Their daddy is big, just like his Greek papa." Ma smiled dreamily when talking about Nik and babies.

No pressure. I groaned.

"Speaking of Nik, how the remodel go? I have great idea for a fountain." Ma pulled out her phone. "I show you."

"No fountains, Ma." I gave her a firm look, but I knew it wouldn't deter her.

Ma lowered her phone and donned a wounded look, but she didn't say she would stop interfering. I honestly didn't think she knew how. Both our Greek mamas had ideas on how to make our home more *Greek*.

"The remodel is going slowly," I continued, letting the matter go for now. "We need to sit down and make some decisions together, but Nik's been a little preoccupied lately with work. You know. Crazy people disturbing the peace, and all." I gave a pointed look in my aunt's direction.

Ma grunted. "You Aunt Tasoula no help it. Day one of reunion they take tour of high school and play the touchy football. Fifty-eight-year-old men squeeze into the old footy ball jerseys. It shameful."

"No more shameful than ancient cheerleaders doing the ancient triangle thingy," Aunt Tasoula chimed in.

"You mean forming a pyramid?" I asked.

"That what I say." She thrust her cutting scissors at me. "They no acute. They afools. They almost break their brittle hips just like cousin, Dimitra." My aunt and Ma made the sign of the cross. "Old bones crack like creaky door with each movement. They have no oil in joints. Then snap, crackle, pop. Never the same again." My aunt's eyes narrowed to slits. "And floozy Skylar shake her pompoms the hardest."

"You just jealous, 'Soula." Ma rolled her eyes.

"What I have to be jealous for? I put on half-time show by myself." My aunt winked at me. "I that good."

"You no that good. You *dangerous*. No one want to be near that crazy flaming baton," Ma pointed out.

"I heard poor eighty-five-year-old former Principal Wimble covered his head and hobbled beneath the bleachers." Leni pressed her lips together, but a giggle still slipped out, earning her a bop on the head from my aunt.

Leni yelped.

"Sit still." Aunt Tasoula shrugged. "No one get hurt this time."

"Until day two at the park," Ma said. "Why you have so many events?"

"What?" my aunt asked but wouldn't quite meet Ma's eyes. "All these people with nice families enjoy Fender's Food Truck and Mr. Chew's Ice Cream stand. The dog park full, and Dino's Daycare supervise so owners can mix the mingle. It was good day. Okay? Okay."

"It *was* okay at beginning," Ma admitted. "Tables in gazebo fill right up to watch bocce ball and crochet competitions. Until you and your nemeses cause drama in ax throwing contest. Then it *no* okay."

"I no help it she crazy fool. She say the ax slip when she swing it over her head to throw forward... only she let go and it sail back to me! She part my teased hair clean down the middle. Do you know how long it took me to get that poof just right?"

"Do *you* know how lucky you are to still have a brain?" Ma asked, then rolled her eyes at me. "I think the ax took some with it."

"Oh, I fine." My aunt waved Ma off. "Day three scavenger hunt around town is perfect. Each clue reveal new location and item to find. We end at Aphrodite's where we eat, drink, and be merry. And there you have it. The end."

"No the end, 'Soula," Ma threw her hands up, "because you just as crazy when you around Skylar."

"I heard the trophy for the winning team got broken," Leni chimed in.

"Because Skylar accuse 'Soula of stacking the teams so she no win." Ma set her jaw. "You two almost broke my statue of Athena, goddess of wisdom and warfare. You lucky I no make war on you."

Aunt Tasoula waved Ma off but was wise enough not to speak.

"Nik told me he put Aunt Tasoula in a time out in Ma's kitchen," I said to Leni whose eyes sprang wide as she covered her mouth with her hand.

"It was either that or a jail cell," Ma clarified.

"I chose dish duty with Frona." My aunt grunted. "Trust me. That punishment enough. That girl a mischievous elf. It take me days to get soap out of my hair."

"Speaking of days," I said. "I heard day four was bowling and quite eventful. You guys should not have played *Never Have I Ever* and *Truth or Dare*. Jaz told me Boomer was called in to break up a fight. Did you actually fight someone?"

"Someone dare Skylar to kiss my Tate...and she did. What you expect?" Aunt Tasoula shrugged.

"I would expect you to behave better on day five," I said and gaped at my aunt in amazement.

"Ah, yes, the movie night," Ma said.

Movie night was held in the high school gym. A large inflatable screen had been rented, and the gym decorated with film reels, old Hollywood props, and movie posters from their graduation year. Movies from forty years ago were played with rows of seats set up to accommodate everyone. Popcorn, candy, soda,

and champagne with the same vintage as their graduation year were served.

Unlike sparkling wine, Aunt Tasoula and Skylar
apparently hadn't gotten better with age.

"I no help it Skylar no hold her alcohol. She get
caramel in my hair and wine on my clothes. It only
fair I do same to her."

"See?" Ma said. "You crazy as her. And now the
school board ban you class from using any school
property again."

"Well, last night go fine, so there you have it." My
aunt kept working on Leni's hair, not quite meeting
Ma's eyes.

Day six had been an evening at their old watering
hole. Back in their day, they were of legal drinking age
their senior year of high school. Rock 'n' Roll Oasis
used to be their haunt, but it now was called Flannigan's Pub.

The owner, Michael Flannigan, was nice enough
to decorate his bar with an eighties theme and all the
attendees came dressed from that decade. They sang
karaoke, played *Name That Tune* for songs from that
era, and told stories from back in the day when they
were in high school.

"No there you have it. Everything fine because
Michael Flannigan smart enough to shut the party
down before you two broke anything." Ma glared at
her sister. "You two need to stop, 'Soula, before something bad happen."

All that was left was the final day...*prom night.*

A re-creation of the early 80s event, with attendees
trying to wear the actual outfits or similar ones, that
they wore from that original night. There would be a
slideshow with pictures from back then, a photo
booth to take current pictures, and the time capsule

they had all made forty years ago would be opened. A disc jockey would play 80s music, and they would dance the night away.

"You worry too much, 'Phelia." My aunt clapped her hands. "Okay, we need to hurry so I get ready. What go wrong on prom night? Everything be okay. You see."

~

ACCORDING to Ma's text messages, the community center was decorated in a starry night theme, with a big mirror ball hanging from the ceiling, and white twinkling lights that reflected off the glass scattered around the room. Silver shiny stars of all sizes hung on different length ribbons from the ceiling while streamers and balloons were draped everywhere. One wall had a starry night photo backdrop with props for pictures, a DJ played 80s music up front by the dance floor, and those who weren't dancing sat at various round tables around the room.

Aphrodite's and Vincenzo's restaurants donated the meals since Ma and Vinny were under a current truce, while Sinfully Delicious bakery provided the desserts. Ma said, so far, everyone had been on their best behavior.

I looked at my phone when a text from my aunt came through, with a picture of her and Tate as the prom king and queen.

"You hear that?" Nik paused, then slid a hammer back into the toolbelt strapped around his jean clad waist.

"Hear what?" I pushed my hard hat back a little so I could see him better.

"Exactly." He smiled, slowly walking over to me as

he pulled his work gloves off and shoved them in his back pocket.

The blissful sound of silence.

For once, our house was quiet. We'd worked all evening on knocking down the rest of the wall separating our apartments. That was the most progress we'd made since we'd returned from our cruise. Wolfgang and Prissy were actually curled up in the same room for once, with neither of them barking or hissing at the other.

Maybe there was hope for us to coexist after all.

I cleared my throat and pulled my own work gloves off, removing my safety glasses. "We still have a lot to discuss."

"Like where to put the fountain your ma wants or the statue my ma does?" His lips twisted into a cockeyed grin.

"Absolutely no to both of those." I folded my hands over my coveralls, standing my ground and changing the subject. "We still have to decide which room we want to use as our master bedroom."

"True, we'll need the other rooms for our eleven children."

I could feel my face pale. "Fur or human?"

He shrugged. "Maybe both."

"Not funny, Detective."

"Have a sense of humor, Ballas. I'm sure they'll all be adopted." His grin faded, replaced with a serious look. "But seriously, do you want children? I know we mentioned it once before, but if we're going to take our relationship to the next level, it's probably something we should discuss."

The word children made my heart speed up. What if I was horrible at being a mother? What if I couldn't handle it? What if that was a deal breaker for Nik?

Knots formed in my stomach. "I agree we have to have that talk, but do we have to have it tonight? It's getting late, and it's been a long day. I'm exhausted."

His eyes softened. "Okay, Ballas, you win." He tweaked my nose. "But we *will* have that talk soon." He paused a beat before adding, "We can't move forward if we aren't on the same page."

I nodded, knowing he was right, but terrified of what would happen if we weren't in fact on the same page. Selfishly, I didn't want to give him up, but could I give him everything he wanted? Was it fair to hold onto him if I couldn't?

"Don't stress, Kalli," he said softly as if reading my thoughts. "We can at least decide on a bed to share, for tonight, anyway." We'd been rotating beds since the start of our relationship. It was half the fun.

I gave him a little smile. "Meet you in mine in ten minutes?"

"Done." He headed into his half of the house, making a beeline for his bathroom as I walked over to mine.

My cell phone rang, stopping me in my tracks. I glanced at the caller ID and blinked.

"Aunt Tasoula? I'm surprised to hear from you. Shouldn't you be at an after party with Tate, or don't they do that anymore?" I asked, curiosity puckering my brow.

"Kalliope, oh woe is me."

My curious grin vanished. "What's wrong?"

Nik must have heard the panic in my voice because he appeared by my side in minutes with a frown on his face.

"The karmama get me. I being paid back."

"Wait, what? You're not making any sense, Aunt Tasoula."

"You come my shop. Then you see. Okay? Okay."

"Right now?" I asked.

Dial tone.

I looked at Nik. "She hung up."

"Grab your coat, Ballas. Let's roll." It was clear he heard our conversation when he slid his gun in its holster and grabbed his own coat, no questions asked. He always had my back.

I loved that about him.

I grabbed my coat and followed him out the door. Ten minutes later we pulled up outside of Hera's Halo and cut the engine. The shop was closed, but all the lights were on. We got out of Nik's car, and he gestured for me to stay behind him. He drew his weapon and carefully swept the area as he made his way inside.

The door was unlocked.

Aunt Tasoula appeared from the back room and let out a scream. "Oh, Detective, you give me fright night. This prom horrible."

"Aunt Tasoula, what is going on?" The feeling of doom settled into my gut.

"Me and Tate, we get into fight. Skylar call him; I say go. I no want him if he want a flake. He leave, so I stab my pastry with fork, clean up mess, and then go home. He lose." She swiped her hands through the air, then dropped them to her sides, her shoulders slumping. "But I no win. I see light on in my shop, so I stop. I never leave light on. That's when the karmama get me."

I rubbed my throbbing temples. "What happened, Aunt Tasoula?"

"Come, come. I show you."

We followed her into her back room and stopped short at the sight before us. My jaw fell open, the doom in my gut churning into a sour volcano. Nik was already making phone calls. Right next to Hera's throne, Skylar Delaney lay on the floor with a pair of Aunt Tasoula's cutting scissors shot straight through her heart, most definitely giving love a bad name. The question was...

Was my aunt to blame?

4

───────

"**Y**ou promised me there wouldn't be any more trouble, Tasoula Cajónes, yet here we are again." Mayor Flynn Zimmerman stood tall and slim with arms folded over her pressed navy-blue suit as she leaned against the table in the Clearview Police Department's interrogation room. Her gray-streaked short hair was styled precisely.

"Tasoula Ballas. Love my Leon, but no like his last name." Aunt Tasoula shuddered. "Cajónes no good."

The mayor just stared at her like she didn't quite know what to do with her. So, she moved on. "I have been listening to complaints all week long from the antics your reunion has caused, *Ms. Ballas.*" She emphasized, and the exasperation in her voice was as clear as Poseidon's tears. "Why couldn't you have planned just one event like most people?"

"I no like most people, and I *no* trouble." Aunt Tasoula stabbed her finger across the table in Tate Hemsworth's direction. "He is. He and that hussy." My aunt was still dressed like an 80s rock band groupie, her hair bigger than Cher's in her prime.

Tate still wore his broad-shouldered tuxedo with tails, sporting a bold red satin cummerbund, bowtie, and scarf. His thick blond hair was parted down the middle and feathered back at the sides. "Skylar is dead, Tasoula. Show some respect."

"Why? She no respect me. *You* no respect me. You leave me for her. That's rude." My aunt crossed her arms, glaring at him.

"What did you expect me to do?" Tate threw his large hands in the air. "She sounded upset when she said she needed help. I couldn't just hang up on her."

"Where did she say she was?" Captain Quincy Crenshaw asked, standing equally as tall as the mayor, but his salt and pepper hair was not as precise as hers. He was still dressed in his suit as well. They'd been out to a business dinner with the town's planning board, discussing the upcoming summer festivals, and were just wrapping up the evening when the call came through about a dead body being found. It was not the early hours of the next morning, and we were all exhausted.

"She didn't say where she was." Tate looked at the captain. "She hung up and didn't answer when I called her back, so I drove around looking for her. I couldn't find her, so I went home. I didn't know what else to do."

Aunt Tasoula scoffed.

"Around what time was that?" Nik asked, sitting beside Boomer while I sat beside my aunt, trying to keep her quiet.

"Skylar called me around nine-thirty, and I drove around for a half hour, so it had to be around ten when I got home. I have a doorbell camera out front that should confirm that. I was too worried to change or go anywhere else, so I just sat there, trying to think of where she might be and how mad Tasoula would be at me." His pleading gaze full of apology shot to my aunt's stubborn angry one.

Her face finally softened, and this time, she didn't look away.

"Do you know of any enemies Skylar may have had?" Nik asked Tate.

Tate scrubbed a hand through his hair then leaned back in his chair. "I really didn't get to know her that well. She did tell me she was recently widowed. Her husband flew his own plane on a business trip, but his plane went down in the ocean a few months ago. She called him her blue-eyed silver fox. I guess he was a lot older than her. This was her fourth marriage. She's never worked. That's about all I know."

"That plenty," my aunt said, waving me off when I tried to shush her. "She move on too fast."

"And when exactly did *you* leave the party, Ms. Ballas?" Boomer asked, looking up at my aunt since she was determined to speak out of turn.

She narrowed her eyes and arched a brow at him. "Don't make me call you mama. She no Greek, but she still a mama."

"I'm just doing my job, Ms. Ballas." Boomer's voice might be neutral, but a bead of sweat appeared at his temple.

Aunt Tasoula hoisted her chin a notch. "I stay until prom over at ten. Then I clean up, so I say ten thirty. I get to my shop around ten forty-five. I call my Kalli by eleven. Then you take me here. Okay? Okay. We good. I go home now?"

"Not just yet, Aunt Tasoula. The detectives need to know anything at all you can think of that might help solve this case." I squeezed her hand.

She nodded. *This crazy. I no like the hussy, but I no*

killer. I patted her hand and let go, praying she wasn't lying.

"Clint Davis, our new medical examiner, put the time of death between ten and eleven." Captain Crenshaw glanced at his notes with a pensive expression, then looked up at Tate. "That means you are free to go, Mr. Hemsworth."

Tate nodded. "What about her?" He pointed toward my aunt.

"Oh, so *now* you care?" She looked away from him, but her words didn't have as much bite this time.

"Do you have cameras that might show what happened in your back room to Mrs. Delaney?" the mayor asked my aunt before Tate could respond.

"Yes." My aunt nodded once.

"Good," the captain said.

"No good." My aunt shook her head.

"Why not?" Boomer scratched his beard.

My aunt shrugged. "They broke."

Nik groaned as he rubbed his forehead. "When?"

She looked off in thought. "Weeks ago...I think."

"Aunt Tasoula, you run a business. You need to protect yourself. Why didn't you get them fixed?" I had gone through far too many antacids per the directions and was a little worried about what that might do to my insides, but the sour sense of doom in my stomach wouldn't go away.

"No time for that." She waved me off like it was no big deal. "I busy planning the reunion. Big job, you know."

"I'm afraid you won't be planning anything in the near future." Nik was all business, but his gaze settled on my aunt.

Aunt Tasoula frowned. "Why?"

"What do you mean *why*?" The mayor paced with

her hands on her hips then stopped abruptly and stared at my aunt, clearly flabbergasted. "You are one exasperating woman. What can't you possibly understand? The victim was killed in your salon with your cutting scissors. It's common knowledge you two are enemies. And you were at the crime scene during the window of time that she was murdered."

"So?" My aunt raised her own hands.

"So," Captain Crenshaw said slowly and carefully to be sure his words sank in, "that means, Tasoula Cajónes Ballas, that unless we find further evidence pointing to someone else, you're our number one suspect."

THE NEXT MORNING, Jaz and I tagged along with Nik and Boomer to the community center. They had a list of everyone who had attended the prom and called them all to meet at the center for questioning. Nik took half and Boomer took the other. No one was allowed to leave town until they were cleared.

"How are the puppies," I asked Jaz as I sipped my tea.

"Big and feisty already. They are growing so quickly, except the runt. I worry a little about her, but the vet says she's perfectly healthy." Jaz ate her pastry and sipped her latte. "I've lined up adopters for just over half of them after they're eight weeks old, but I'm worried we'll still have ten of them left."

"It's early yet. We still have time." I couldn't even think about taking on my half. That would mean five, and with my luck, they would take after big ole' slobbery Wolfy. My stomach flipped over the mere thought of more slobber in my house. I'd already made Wolfgang several bibs, but he'd chewed them all.

Yet another reason why I was dragging my feet a little on finishing the remodel.

My gaze traveled over to my detective, and my heart melted. He was the reason I'd knocked a hole in the wall in the first place, but once the remodel was finished, living together would become real. The cruise we had taken together had confirmed I would do anything for this man. He *got* me. Quirks and all, he loved me. And he was helping me to love myself. But could he *live* with me? That was the thing I most worried about.

After what felt like hours, the men finally joined us at our table.

"Any luck?" Jaz asked them before they were even settled in their seats.

"Most of the guests went to the after party and alibied out," Boomer said, scanning his notes.

"But we did have a few who don't have anyone to confirm their alibis and they definitely have motive," Nik added.

"First off, Chelsea Turner was a fellow cheerleader back in high school." Boomer flipped to a page in his notebook. "She lost out on being captain to Sklyar and never got over it. Apparently, she was always jealous of her and still is. She never married and has worked as a flight attendant for decades. Skylar belittled her in front of everyone, and she stormed out of Prom just before Skylar left."

"Where did she go?" Jaz asked.

"Says she drove to Lakeshore Heights just across the town line because she didn't want to stay at the same hotel as Skylar. Of course, the owner doesn't have cameras." Boomer grunted. "It's in the woods with cabins on the lake. It's totally remote, and all sorts of shady stuff goes down there, but he's always booked full."

"Because the owner turns a blind eye and shady people know that." Nik shook his head. "What else you got?"

"Grant Kingsley."

Jaz's eyes widened. "The movie star?" She swatted Boomer's arm. "Why didn't you tell me he was in town?"

Boomer rubbed his arm and frowned. "Because I didn't know. He used an alias at the hotel. Why do you care? You don't need a movie star." He sat up straighter and puffed out his chest. "You have me."

She rolled her eyes. "You know you're my hero, but it would have been nice to meet an official one in person."

Boomer narrowed his eyes. "Nice save, Alvarez. I'm only letting you off the hook because the man is old enough to be your father."

"So are any of the James Bonds, but they're still dreamy." She winked and pretended to swoon.

He scowled. "Anyway. Grant was a tall, gangly nerd with glasses in high school. He had a crush on Skylar back then, but she shot him down. Now he's a regular Clark-Kent-turned-into-Superman. The dude's jacked now, and far from nerdy. This time Skylar came onto him, and he was only too happy to give her a taste of her own medicine by turning her down in front of everyone. He never showed up at the afterparty or his hotel. Said he drove around and ended up at The Lookout. That was a make out place their class used to go to. Kids still do today, but he said he fell asleep in his car, so he doesn't know if anyone saw him."

"Do you believe him?" Nik asked.

"Not for a minute," Boomer said.

"Wow, their graduating class was full of rebellious people, yet my aunt and Ma used to lecture me about mine," I said, then I remembered something. "Hey, what about Ursula Smith? My aunt said something about her being class president and mad because she wasn't the one to plan the reunion. I guess that's how high school reunions usually work. I wouldn't know. I never went to my tenth."

"Too bad, Ballas." Nik grinned. "Mine was a blast. You know. Catching up with old *friends* and all."

"Hmmm," was all I said. I could only imagine how many *friends* Detective Dreamy had back in high school.

"I have to admit, ours was pretty fun, but neither of these fine women went," Boomer pointed out. "Guess they were too cool for school."

"Who needs friends when you have a bestie like mine?" Jaz winked at me.

"Exactly." I smiled at Jaz then turned to Boomer, ignoring a chuckling Nik. "Time's wasting, Detective."

"Right." Boomer resumed where he left off. "Ursula was present at all the disruptions during the week. Maybe she was trying to sabotage your aunt by pitting Skylar against her." Boomer looked at his notes again. "She would certainly know how to cover her tracks if she was trying to set your aunt up for killing Skylar. She was the valedictorian in high school, graduated college Summa cum laude, and is a high-powered defense attorney today. She says she was with her girlfriend, and they rented an Airbnb on the outskirts of town. Her girlfriend confirms she was with her, but she could just be covering for her."

"Anything else?" Nik asked.

Boomer scanned his notes a final time and turned to Nik. "That's it for me, partner. How about you?"

Nik pulled out his own notebook. "Drake Fontana. He was a rebel bad boy in high school, always getting into trouble. In and out of foster care growing up, he quit high school and taught himself how to cook from cooking shows on TV. He's a top chef these days and owns a chain of restaurants."

"What does he have to do with Skylar's murder?" I asked.

"Well, apparently, she was mad that he was at the reunion. She was a member of the student counsel in high school and planned a lot of events that Drake ruined. She said he didn't graduate; therefore, he wasn't officially part of their class and had no business being at prom. Drake got angry. He has a temper like that famous chef, Gordon Ramsay. Drake and Skylar got into a shouting match just before she left, and he stormed out moments later."

"Where did he go?" I asked.

"His friend who still lives in town is gone on vacation and letting him stay at his place so he can try out some new recipes. No cameras there either, and no one to validate his alibi." Nik shrugged.

"A little too convenient if you ask me." Boomer rubbed his jaw.

"Maybe." Nik flipped the page in his notebook. "Next up, we have Hannah Schwarts. She was always the class clown and is now a stand-up comedian. She runs a comedy club in NYC. Skylar used to bully her, and Hannah used to cover up her depression with humor. Back in high school, she was too afraid to stand up for herself. Not so much now. Apparently, she did an impromptu standup act at prom, making Skylar the butt of her jokes this time. Skylar was furious."

I groaned. "I bet Aunt Tasoula loved every minute of that."

"Hannah claims she stayed with her sister, Helen, and they had a girls' night to catch up. Her sister confirmed her alibi, but her neighbor's camera showed them leaving the house at ten and not coming back until eleven. They said they went on a spontaneous run through the cemetery, like they did when they were kids, to scare each other. They were watching horror movies all night long. And of course, there are no cameras posted around the graves in the cemetery out of respect."

"So, what you're saying is that, unless a ghost can confirm her alibi, she's still a suspect," Jaz concluded.

"Correct." Nik nodded.

"Anyone else?" Boomer asked.

"One couple. Malik and Keisha Cooper. Apparently, he was prom king and Skylar's former boyfriend back in high school. He played football and wrestled, while Skylar was head cheerleader."

"I would think Skylar would be thrilled to reminisce with him," Jaz said. "Relive their glory days."

"She was, but his *wife* wasn't so thrilled," Nik went on, flipping another page in his notes. "He married a woman who played soccer and rugby in college. They own a gym and have four sons and a bunch of grandchildren, but they look like they are twenty years younger. Skylar wouldn't stop flirting with Malik, even though she was there with these French brothers ten years her junior."

"They are the ones she met earlier this week in Aphrodite's," I said. "Aunt Tasoula sent me a bunch of pictures of the evening and her winning prom queen."

"They told people at prom that they were in town for the spring festival, but this reunion sounded like fun, so they said yes to accompanying Skylar when she asked them. Anyway, Keisha publicly threatened Skylar to back off from her husband or she would be sorry, then she stabbed her steak with a knife."

"Oh, boy," I said.

"Oh, yeah," Nik agreed. "He's pretty calm, but his wife could use an anger management class. They're big campers, so they drove their camper to Clearview Campgrounds and stayed there. Not many people are camping yet, so no one was by their lot to confirm if they went straight there after prom. That's all I have for now."

"Well, that's better than none." I nodded, determined to find a way to clear my aunt's name. She would never be able to handle prison. "That's at least six people who had motive and have no confirmable alibi. If only we can place them at Hera's Halo somehow, then my aunt will be off the hook."

"Then let's get to work." Jaz stood.

"Wait, there is no *us*." Nik looked at Boomer before leveling his serious icy blue gaze on me. "You're far too close to this case, Kalli. It's your aunt we're talking about. Please listen to me and stay out of this one."

"Exactly. It's my family, Nik. I'm not just going to sit by and watch her go to jail for a crime she didn't commit." I eyed him with my determined green gaze and lowered my voice. "I *heard* her claim her innocence."

Nik sighed. "I don't doubt your aunt, or what you heard, Ballas. But I can't do a thing about it unless you can prove it."

And therein lay the problem.

5

That afternoon, the sky was overcast. The forecast called for rain, but so far, not a single raindrop had fallen. I drove around town until I spotted Chelsea Turner's car. She was parked at Diner Delights, so I pulled into the parking lot and went inside. The deli belonged to my cousins, Kosmos and Silas.

Kosmos was short and intimidating, built like a tank but was really a big soft teddy bear inside. He was dating our mail carrier, Winnie, who looked like an Amazon warrior with an Australian accent. He'd been like warm honey in her hands from the moment he met her. Kosmos made the food while Silas took the orders and ran the register. Silas was tall with curly black hair and dimples. He was still charming but was no longer the town flirt since Zena, the petite pixie blond bartender at Flannigan's Pub, had taken him off the market.

That meant only one thing...the Greek mamas were getting bored.

Bored mamas meant mayhem for sure. Everyone except my cousin Leni and brother Jasper were spoken for. The mamas had been struck with spring fever and were on a mission before murder had put a pause to the matchmaking.

"Hey, Kalli, what can I get you?" Silas asked with a wink. He stood behind the counter with his apron on and a hat on his head, looking as handsome as ever.

"I'll take a Greek salad and an iced tea." I dug through my backpack purse until I found what I was looking for, then with a tissue of course, I set cash on the counter. There were so many germs on dollar bills, my skin crawled just thinking about it. But I had some cash I needed to use up.

Silas shook his head, chucking over my tissue, as he took the twenty. "You're one of a kind, cuz."

"Yes, I am, and I'm proud of it." I laughed.

"Your order's comin' right up, cousin," Kosmos hollered from behind the counter as he got to work on my order. "And don't listen to my knucklehead brother. You're perfect just the way you are."

"Thanks, cousin, now tell me what you want." I raised a brow at him. He was a serious man normally. Flattery wasn't one his of strengths.

"She got you, bro." Silas punched him on the arm.

Kosmos looked down at his arm and then leveled a glare at Silas. "I'm twice your size. You really wanna go there, *bro*?"

"Touché" Silas backed away with his hands up in dramatic fashion, but the grin never left his face.

Kosmos's face melted into a pleading expression when he looked at me. "Help me pick out a six-month anniversary present for Winnie? I have no clue what I'm doing, and I want her to feel special."

"Awe." My heart filled with tenderness for my tough-as-nails cousin. I'd never seen him insecure or vulnerable before.

"Hey, I offered to help him, but for some reason, he doesn't like my taste." Silas dropped his hands to his waist. "Says I'm inappropriate, whatever that means."

"Gee, I can't imagine," I said dryly and rolled my eyes at Silas, then turned to his brother. "Of course, I'll help you, Kosmos. Text me when you have some free time, and we'll catch up. I have a few ideas." I planned to design some extra special Kalli Original lingerie just for Winnie that I knew would flatter her gorgeous Amazon warrior physique. She would love it. I smiled a little. And I suspected Kosmos would love it just as much.

"I owe you." Kosmos saluted me then got to work on finishing my order, the heavenly smells coming from his kitchen making my mouth water.

I looked around as I waited, spotting Dino Willis of Dino's Doggie Daycare at a table with a striking woman. Since taking Wolfgang to daycare, I'd gotten to know Dino pretty well. He was a nice enough guy, but a little quiet and socially awkward. I could relate, although I'd come a long way since dating Nik.

Dino was on the thin side, with curly auburn hair, brown eyes, and glasses. I'd never seen him with a woman before. She had a black silky bob of hair with light brown highlights streaked through, dressed in leather, and sporting a metal choker necklace. He seemed focused on her every word.

Go Dino.

Maybe a relationship would help him, too. He caught me staring, so I smiled at him, and he blushed before waving quickly then looking away. I kept my gaze moving around the diner until I spotted Chelsea Turner. Once my food was ready, I grabbed my salad and tea and made my way over to her table.

"Do you mind if I sit with you?" I asked with a friendly smile.

She eyed me warily. "Suit yourself." Her hair was a pretty silver that fell naturally in waves to her shoulders.

"I'm Kalli." I sat down and hung my backpack on the back of my seat.

"I know who you are. I saw you at the community center with the detectives." She studied me. "You don't look anything like your family."

"I'm adopted."

"Look, I'm sure you're probably trying to clear your aunt's name, but I didn't have anything to do with Skylar's murder."

"I'm not here to say that you did. I'm just trying to understand everything that happened. I know my aunt never cared for Skylar back in high school. You cheered with her, right? What was she like back then?"

"We might have been on the same team, but we were still competitors. Anything Skylar wanted she found a way to get. Boys, head cheerleader, grades. It wasn't fair. She was failing math. She shouldn't have even been eligible to be on the team." Chelsea leaned forward and lowered her voice. "Suddenly, right before tryouts, she has an A. The math ain't mathin' if you ask me."

"It definitely doesn't seem to add up. How is that possible?"

"Having a teacher like Jack Harris." Chelsea sat back and sipped her lemonade. "Skylar always did like older men."

My jaw hit the floor. Jack had to be seventy and was retired now, but he was a well-respected family man on the school board these days. "I'm shocked," I said. "My aunt never mentioned anything like that. Ma either."

"I'm not surprised. They kept a pretty low profile, but I knew all about it. I also knew Skylar would ruin me if I told anyone, so I kept my mouth shut and missed out on what was rightfully mine. He was single at the time of the indiscretion, and Skylar was eighteen, but sleeping with a student in exchange for good grades was still unethical." Chelsea's face twisted into a disgusted expression.

"Even all these years later, that will ruin him if it gets out." He was always commissioning special orders from me. Now I had to wonder if they were for his wife or someone else.

"He shouldn't be allowed to stay on the school board. I should have said something years ago, but I was afraid no one would believe me. I didn't have any proof other than Skylar bragging to the girls about it. She makes me sick. She always got her way back then." Chelsea's face transformed into a satisfied smile. "But not this time."

"What was that?"

Chelsea blinked, as if realizing she'd spoken out loud. "I just mean, it was satisfying seeing people stand up to her for once. Her late husband was barely cold in the sea, yet she was at the reunion with men she just met, then she hit on her ex-boyfriend Malik right in front of his wife. I wanted to stand up and clap when Grant shot her down, but Hannah beat me to the punch line by roasting her with a little stand-up."

"I heard about that."

"I thought Drake was going to burst a blood vessel, he was so mad at Skylar. I don't wish anyone dead, but I do believe in karma."

"It certainly sounds like it was quite the trip down

memory lane. How come you didn't go to the after party?"

"Let's just say, I found other ways to entertain myself."

～

THAT EVENING I stopped by Aphrodite's to grab dinner to go for Nik, Boomer, Jaz, and me. Nik was at the station going over notes with Boomer, while Jaz was home on puppy duty. I had already fed my fur babies, so I was the only one free.

I didn't mind. I wanted to check on my aunt. Since my aunt's salon was a crime scene and closed temporarily, she was helping out my parents at the restaurant. I kept having the strangest feeling of being watched. It was already dark outside, as the days hadn't grown longer yet. I shut my car off and, after one last glance around the parking lot to be sure I was alone, I quickly went inside the restaurant.

Jasper was handy and did most repairs for Ma, but sometimes the job called for two people. "Hi, Kalli, nice to see you again." Vicky stepped inside the restaurant, wearing her standard toolbelt.

"Same to you," I said with a smile. I really liked her energy. "I take it you're here to help Jasper?"

"Yup. Third time this week. Your mother keeps finding jobs that *just can't wait*." She laughed.

I was glad she could find humor in the situation. "You do know she's trying to fix you up with my brother, don't you?" I arched an eyebrow.

"I figured as much." She shrugged. "It's okay. People do that to me all the time. They think I need to be taken care of." She winked. "Until I show them all I can do by my little ole' self."

"I bet you do." I laughed. "With Ma, it's more like she wants someone to take care of her little boy." I rolled my eyes.

Vicky's gaze drifted over to Jasper. "Um, he doesn't look so little to me or like he needs to be taken care of."

"Exactly." I laughed.

Jasper spotted us. He waved to me then motioned her over.

"Guess that's my cue." She saluted me and made a beeline for Jasper with a no-nonsense gait.

I made my way to the kitchen, passing Grant Kingsley with his wife, children, and nanny sitting in a booth in the far corner. His wife was decades younger than him and quite beautiful with her platinum blond hair and sky-blue eyes. I'd seen pictures of them on TV, so I knew it was his family, but that still didn't stop the people of Clearview from asking for autographs. He seemed to like it, reveling in the attention.

His wife, not so much.

Grant pasted on a Hollywood smile as he accommodated them. I couldn't help wondering what he was hiding behind that million-dollar smile. If only he'd gone to the hotel with his wife instead of The Lookout alone, then he would have an alibi.

I headed toward my cousin Leni to see if my order was ready yet. She was taking Clint Davis's order. He was staring up at her with his mesmerizing whiskey-colored eyes, his smile making the cleft in his chin look even deeper.

I started heading her way. I wanted to catch her when she was finished, before she disappeared into the kitchen, but a movement out of the corner of my eye distracted me. I paused. Ma was flapping her arms like a loon on the lake, and I knew from experience she wouldn't stop until I went over to see what she wanted.

"I got you," Ma said. "Leni busy with the medical examiner. Maybe he examine her." She waggled her eyebrows at me and grinned wide.

"Are you matchmaking again, Ma?" I pointed my finger at her.

She swatted my finger away. "What? He a good-looking man. Tall, dark, and handsome. I bet he part Greek. They would make beautiful Greek babies. But he no make a move. If he no hurry up, Blondie at next table steel her away. He definitely no Greek."

"Ma..." I looked at who she was talking about, and it was the man with the blond hair who'd sat next to me in my aunt's hair salon. He was alone again, eating his meal, reading another newspaper. Leni stopped at his table next, and he smiled up at her, flashing those dimples once more.

"See." She pointed when Leni smiled back at him. "Some people need help." Ma grunted. "You *still* do. Now take this to you man so he want to make Greek babies with you."

"Ma!" I was amazed that she could still surprise me after all these years, yet she did time and again. "We're not even married yet."

"*Yet*?" She sucked in a breath. "Did he propose?"

"Yes," I paused and watched her eyes bug, "he proposed we eat dinner before we starve to death."

"You a bad girl, Kalliope." She shook her head at me. "Now, hurry before it go cold. Nikos and Boomer need they strength." A twinkle entered her eye. "You feed him well, then he *propose* you make Greek babies."

One. Track. Mind.

I rolled my eyes and changed the subject. "How's Aunt Tasoula?"

"Oh, woe is me. She no good. Her salon ruined. Her man gone. Now she talking to new man. Clayton Brown. He older and distinguished. She trying to make Tate like jelly. He no soft and jelly, he hard and angry. She drive me crazy. You detectives need to find the real killer, Tonto."

"You mean pronto?"

"That's what I say. Now go." A crash sounded in the kitchen.

I winced. "Frona breaking dishes again?"

"You aunt much worse than her." Ma held the back of her hand to her forehead. "*My* restaurant be ruined soon if she no leave."

And the Oscar goes to Ophelia Ballas.

"Oh, boy." I played along. "Thanks for the food, Ma."

"Go, go." She waved me off and shuffled back into the kitchen, uttering I-didn't-want-to-know-what in Greek. When she spoke that fast, I couldn't keep up, but I was pretty sure I wouldn't want to hear what she said anyway.

I left the restaurant and dropped off dinner at the police station in record time. Ten minutes after that, I arrived at Jaz and Boomer's apartment.

I knocked on the door, but there was no answer.

I knocked again, but still no answer.

This time I pounded on the door.

Finally, Jaz opened the door with sleepy eyes, looking around a little disoriented. She stepped back and let me in. Her clothes were wrinkled, her hair a mess, her make-up smudged. I'd never seen her this disheveled.

"Wow, you really must be exhausted." I walked inside and set the food on the kitchen table. "You took a nap without even changing out of your work clothes. That's so unlike you."

"Yes. No. I don't know." She looked down as if just now realizing she hadn't changed her clothes like she normally did as she followed me into the kitchen. "I left work and came right home to relieve Milly because I knew Boomer was working. I don't remember anything else except waking up on the couch right now when you started pounding. I didn't have a pillow or blanket or anything. I was just tipped over on the couch." She sat in a chair and rubbed her head. "I feel like I have the biggest hangover, yet I didn't touch a drop."

"Sleep exhaustion will do that to you."

She frowned. "This is weird. Something's wrong."

"It's because it's quiet. Enjoy it while it lasts."

Her eyes sprang wide. "With twenty-two puppies and two mamas, it's never quiet. Someone is always up needing something." She surged to her feet and ran over to the guest bedroom then stopped short and gasped.

"What's wrong?" I held my breath.

"They're gone," she answered in barely more than a whisper.

My heart started racing. "How many?"

She turned to face me; her complexion paler than a ghost. "All of them. Someone stole all of the puppies, and their mamas, too. They've been puppy-napped." She started to pace then stopped and looked at me with wide dazed eyes that were starting to fill with tears. "What are we going to do?"

I grabbed my keys and backpack then took her by

the arm. "The first thing we're going to do is get you to Doc LaLone's office, because I think you're right. Something is most definitely wrong." I studied her eyes as we headed to my car. "I think you've been drugged."

6

I didn't like hospitals or doctors, but I trusted Doc LaLone. The man was in his sixties, with thick white hair, a stethoscope, and a white lab coat. He was old school like me and had been my doctor for my entire life. His wife Joan was his nurse, and his daughter Cindy was his receptionist.

He was the only doctor who had never made me feel like a freak.

"I suspect Kalli's right, Jaz. You weren't sleeping. You were drugged. Everything I'm seeing indicates that the tests we took will confirm that. Someone must have slipped a sedative into your drink before you headed home," Doc LaLone said, lowering the little flashlight he'd been shining in her eyes.

Jaz rubbed her head. "That could have been anyone. My coffee was right out in the open. Anyone in my store would have had access to it. And I didn't take a sip until I left the store, so it hit me just after I got home."

"Like you said, Jaz, these puppies are in high demand," I pointed out. "The spring festival is going on, and there are a lot of people in town. We have signs about adopting them posted all over. With Boomer working the murder investigation, he's not around much, making you an easy target."

"I'm just glad this didn't happen when Milly was there. She's in her last trimester." A tear slipped out of Jaz's eye and rolled down her cheek. "I never would have forgiven myself if something bad happened to her or her baby because of me. Poor Chanel and Versace. My girls are going to be so confused and wonder where I am. You don't think whoever has them will hurt my dogs or the puppies, do you?"

I was already shaking my head. "They're worth too much money alive."

She twisted the material at the bottom of her blouse. "How am I going to tell Boomer? He's going to be so upset."

I took her hand. "We'll do it together."

"Okay. Can we do it now? I don't want to wait any longer."

"If it's okay with Doc." I looked at him for an answer.

He nodded, so we gathered our things and left.

Fifteen minutes later, Jaz and I walked through the front door to the police station, carrying our dinner.

"Can we use your microwave?" I asked Nik.

He arched a thick, black eyebrow at me. "Sure, but we're working, you know. Is something wrong with Jaz's microwave?"

"Well, no, but we didn't want to disturb any evidence," I said.

"Evidence that Jaz can't cook?" Boomer smirked. "That's already been established, and I'm marrying her anyway."

Jaz burst into tears.

Boomer rushed to her side and took her in his

arms. "Hey, babe, I was just teasing you. I love to cook. We'll be fine."

She was already shaking her head. "You don't understand," she said into his shirt. "We won't be fine because our babies are gone."

He stilled.

"Babies?" Boomer looked at Nik over the top of her head.

Nik shrugged, looking to me.

"Chanel, Versace, and all of their twenty-two puppies were puppy-napped," I explained, feeling the length of the exhausting day suddenly hit me.

"I'm confused. How could anyone steal them? Aren't they always being watched?" Nik asked.

Jaz stepped out of Boomer's arms, and I handed her a tissue. "I came straight home from work to relieve Milly, but I passed out shortly after stepping inside. I didn't wake up until a couple hours later when Kalli pounded on our door."

"How is that even possible?" Boomer asked. "You literally wake up at a single whimper. Your mom-dar is off the charts."

"Because she was drugged," I clarified.

"What?" Boomer grabbed Jaz's shoulders and looked into her eyes. "Are you okay, Babe? We need to get you to the doctors right now."

"I'm fine," she said. "We just came from there. Doc thinks it was a sedative. The tests he took will tell us exactly which one. Someone must have slipped it into my drink while I was working."

"That's so dangerous. You're lucky you didn't crash while driving under the influence on the way home," Nik pointed out.

Boomer balled his fists and began to pace. "Who would do this?"

"We need to send a team over to your place to sweep your apartment for evidence." Nik picked up his cell and made the call.

"Two full-sized poodles and twenty-two puppies. That's a lot of animals. Someone had to have seen something, don't you think?" I asked.

"Not necessarily," Boomer said. "We're on the ground floor and there's a back entrance to our building. I'll check with our landlord and see if anything show's up on the cameras." A muscle in his jaw bulged. "Clearly, whoever it was knew what they were doing and timed this just right."

"Call Thalia." Jaz rubbed her arms. "We need to hurry up and find a house. I don't feel comfortable in that apartment now."

"I will. I promise. Right now, in fact. I don't want you staying there, period." Boomer pulled out his phone to send Thalia a text.

"In the meantime," I said, "why don't you both stay with us for a couple days. As long as you don't mind the disarray, we both have guest bedrooms."

"If you're sure you don't mind, we'll take you up on that," Jaz said. "I can't bear to look into that empty puppy pen right now. Is that okay, Boomer?"

"Whatever makes you comfortable. Nik and I will be working most of the time anyway." Boomer shot Nik a glance. "Is that okay with you, buddy?"

"Absolutely." Nik's eyes found mine. "We haven't made any permanent decisions yet anyway, so the girls can take Kalli's half, and you can bunk up at mine. It'll be just like old times."

"Minus one very significant wall between the two apartments," I pointed out, but I had to admit I felt a little relieved that the pressure to make decisions was put on pause temporarily. I wanted to finish our remodel and make a home with Nik more than anything, but I wanted everything to be perfect.

"It's settled then," Nik said with a tone I didn't quite recognize as his eyes locked with mine. "I guess the remodel can wait."

Suddenly, I wondered how long *he* would be willing to wait, and just like that, the terrible sense of doom settled in my stomach once more.

~

THE NEXT MORNING, I let Jaz sleep in. Nik and Boomer were already gone to the station. Prissy and Wolfgang were on their best behavior, almost as if they sensed something was up with Jaz. The wall between our apartments was still gone, but the open space didn't make it seem like one home. It still had the feel of two entirely different apartments except we could see and hear what everyone was doing.

I wasn't sure I liked this pause.

A pause felt like we were taking a step back for some reason. I needed a distraction, so I grabbed my list and backpack then headed out the door to Stallone's Supermarket. Salvatore Stallone's widow had changed the name from Sal's to Stallone's, but everything else was still the same. A mom-and-pop grocery store, with all the staples and a few unique items that no one else carried. That's what made this store a gem to anyone who liked to cook.

I put my list and pack in a shopping cart and headed down the first row, browsing the shelves and picking up each item I needed as I spotted it. I picked up a few more items that weren't on my list. Sal's widow had put her spin on the store, adding items Sal probably never would have thought of.

I turned down the next row, stopping short before I ran into a man standing in the middle of the aisle, squinting.

"Pop?" My jaw fell open. "What are you doing here?" He had food trucks deliver to the restaurant, and Ma did the shopping for home, so what on earth was my pop doing shopping for himself?

He turned toward me, and his face lit up. "Oh, my Kalliope. You good girl."

"Thanks, Pop. I try."

Pop drew his eyebrows together. "You mama and you aunt, they no good." He shook his still thick gray head of hair. "They crazy. I get out of there." He scrubbed his hands over his face.

"What did they do now?" I wasn't entirely sure I wanted to know, but Pop looked a little lost and desperate.

"I get my superglue and duct tape from Tate's Hardware, but you aunt no let me go there now," he whined. "Where I suppose to go now. She never think of me. It all about her. It always all about her. She parading around with her new man, Clayton. What kind of name is Clayton. He no Greek."

Neither was Tate.

My pop made an exception for him. He didn't like that Tate first dated Ma back in high school before she met him. But Pop figured Tate dating Aunt Tasoula was a good thing, so the man would leave Ma alone. And Pop liked Tate's hardware store.

Pop just didn't like change.

I reached up to the top shelf and pulled down some duct tape and superglue. "Here you go, Pop."

He clapped his hands. "What I do without you?" I hugged him. *Now if only you give me nice Greek grandbabies before you get too old, I be a happy papou.*

I quickly dropped my arms. Oh, my Zeus, I couldn't handle my Pop pressuring me, too. "Well, I have to get going. Jaz and Boomer are staying with us for a little while, so I have to get some groceries."

"Oh, I hear all about the babies getting napped. I thought babies supposed to nap." He scratched his head. "I guess *this* napping is bad. You mama and aunt want to be like Pink Panther and catch the nappers. I say no pink. Everyone see them coming. They hard to miss, you know. What do I know?"

"Tell me they won't do anything reckless, please." I groaned.

"I tell them to stay out of trouble. They no listen. I tell you, they as crazy as the Greek Goddess Hera. They stubborn and manipulate men. Anything to get they own way." He looked at me, as if startled he'd spoken that part out loud. "Don't tell them I say so. They send me to Hades if you do."

"My lips are sealed." I pretended to zip them and throw away the key.

He squinted at my lips. "Try some Aloe. Aloe good for everything. There you have it." He nodded. "Aloe must be Greek. Did you know—"

"Gotta go, Pop." I waved and left the aisle quickly.

I finished the rest of my shopping in record time and was almost to my car when I heard voices in the parking lot. I hid my cart and ducked behind the nearest car then peeked through the window to listen.

Drake Fontana and Ursula Smith were standing between their cars talking.

Drake had shoulder-length brown hair pulled back into a short ponytail, and a goatee that was fully gray. Ursula was taller than him, with snow white hair buzzed tight to her head in stark contrast to her caramel skin tone. Drake's hands moved as he talked, while Ursula calmly stood there with her arms crossed.

"Look, I did everything you asked me to do last time." Drake thrust his finger in Ursula's face. "If you didn't like the results, you should have found someone else to do the leg work. I can't help it you're incapable of holding up your end."

"Oh, I'm more than capable. I guess I just expected a little more professionalism from you." She looked at him with disgust. "Why would you leave the scissors there? That was an amateur move."

His jaw flexed, and he took a deep breath as if counting to ten. "I admit, that was a mistake."

"A rookie mistake," she ground out.

He raised his voice. "You could have done the job yourself, you know. This isn't my thing."

She put her hands on her hips but kept her voice level. "Well, I didn't, and now we're in too deep."

"*We* aren't in too anything, princess."

"I'm *not* taking the fall alone." Her gaze hardened. "Consider yourself warned if you leave me hanging."

"I told you that was a one and done. This is why I work solo. I don't need this kind of drama." He looked a little wary. "I'm out." He climbed into his car, slammed the door, and peeled away.

"You can come out now, Ms. Ballas," Ursula said, her eyes shooting like lasers in my direction.

I sucked in a sharp breath. How did she know I was there? I carefully stood. "Sorry, I dropped my quarter."

She arched a brow. "And you spent five minutes looking for it?"

"What can I say, it was my lucky quarter, but it's gone forever now." I sighed dramatically, channeling

Ma and Aunt Tasoula. I cleared my throat. "I couldn't help overhearing your conversation."

"Really, now?" she said dryly.

I gave up the charade. "If you know something about Skylar Delaney's murder, you need to talk to Detective Stevens."

"I don't *need* to do anything, Ms. Ballas. I know my rights. You're going to have to do better than that."

"If you have nothing to hide, wouldn't you want to help solve a friend's murder?" I was trying anything at this point.

Ursula laughed harshly. "Skylar was no friend of mine."

I paused a beat to let my words sink in. "Neither was my aunt, apparently."

Ursula lifted one shoulder in a shrug. "I didn't dislike your aunt, but I definitely didn't like her stepping on my toes. I should have been the one to plan this reunion. It's customary for the senior class president to do so. Your aunt wasn't an officer of our graduating class whatsoever."

"My aunt lives in town, while you don't," I tried to explain and smooth things over. "She was only trying to help."

A harsh laugh slipped out of Ursula's mouth. "And look how that turned out, my dear. Not so swell."

"The truth will come out, you know." I held her gaze. "It always does."

She held mine right back. "I'm counting on it."

7

"Aunt Tasoula, what are you doing?" I waved her over to a tree in Clearview Park that afternoon.

The temperature had warmed up nicely with a warm breeze carrying the smell of grass, flowers, and pine with it. The sun had been shining earlier, but a few clouds had rolled in. I refused to let them dampen the day. I was trying to distract Jaz from the missing puppies by taking her to the Spring Festival while Nik and Boomer investigated Skylar's murder as well as the puppy-napping and the counterfeit money incidents.

My crazy aunt was definitely a distraction.

"Why you two hiding in tree?" Aunt Tasoula squinted at us while wearing a tight, sparkly majorette costume from the 80s.

"We're not hiding. There's nowhere to sit," Jaz pointed out.

"You've taken up all the picnic tables." I stared in disbelief, gesturing behind her to a scene that was stealing the show.

Clayton Brown, the older gentleman I had thought she was seeing exclusively, sat at one table patiently waiting with a baton in his hand. At another table sat the French brothers, Antoine and Louis Dupont, looking confused as they talked with their hands and pointed multiple times at the two batons on the table in front of them. Then there was Drake Fontana, looking downright perturbed, tapping yet another baton on the wood.

Malik Cooper and Grant Kingsley were both married. Otherwise, I was sure she would have them sitting at even more tables. Finally, poor Tate sat alone, scowling, with no baton anywhere near him.

I looked at my aunt, waiting for her explanation.

"What? I hand out batons to my suitors." Aunt Tasoula smoothed her fancy updo. "They all want me, you know. They can't help themselves."

"So, that's why you're wearing that outfit?" I shook my head. "Aunt Tasoula, you're not the bachelorette."

"Of course not, silly." She shrugged. "I the majorette." She winked. "They all want my batons. Much better than pompoms."

I eyed the confused looking men with a raised eyebrow. "*Do they?*"

"Of course, they do. Who wouldn't?" She ran a hand down the sequins of her costume. "I fabulous."

"You nincompoop is what you are." Ma marched over to us, her hands moving in time with her feet. "What you think you doing?"

Aunt Tasoula struck a pose. "I majoretting."

"They call it something else in my day." Ma grunted with a big eye roll. "You no go around dating all these men at same time. You crazy, 'Soula. You the main suspect in murder investigation. How 'bout you worry about that." Ma thrust her pointer finger at my aunt. "*Not* you love life."

"Murder Shmurder. I innocent." Aunt Tasoula crossed her arms stubbornly. "And I having fun."

"And *I* could use help at food tent, Ms. America." Ma pointed over to the long line at Aphrodite's.

Aunt Tasoula let out a trilling giggle and beamed a smile at my ma. "You really think I win beauty pageant? I *am* talented." She twirled in a circle and tossed her baton high, which hit the tree then ricocheted into Ma's beehive like cupid's arrow.

Ma was most definitely not feeling the love.

Aunt Tasoula's eyes grew huge. "Good thing for you I no use fire. You hive burn up like Principal Wimble's rug hair."

"Good thing for *you* we in public." Ma poked my aunt in the chest, and I could have sworn there was steam hissing from her red ears.

My aunt let out a yelp and clutched her chest as if she'd been shot, drawing several sets of eyes in our direction.

"Cut the act, 'Soula. You no getting out of helping me." Ma yanked the baton out of her beehive and thrust it at her sister with several frizzy strands attached. "You *owe* me."

Aunt Tasoula stopped clutching her chest and took the baton, heaving out a sigh. "You so dramatic, Ophelia. Of course, I help. We family." She started to follow Ma without so much as a backward glance at all the men waiting for her.

"You're just going to leave them sitting there alone with your batons?" I sputtered, amazed at my aunt's boldness.

"I a mystery," she said over her shoulder with a wave at the men and a wink for me, swinging her hips like a pendulum at high speed as she clickety clacked her way over to Aphrodite's food tent.

"I don't even know what to say." Jaz looked at me with wide eyes.

"There are no words." I shook my head.

Now that the distraction was over with, I tried to think of what we should do next. Eat food, play games, watch a show. A rumble of thunder sounded way off in the distance. I glanced at the sky which had grown a little darker, and an ominous feeling of doom swept over me once more. I tightened my backpack as I scanned the crowd of people with an uneasy feeling settling in my gut.

Maybe you should call it a day and leave before anything else bad happens, whispered through my brain.

"Oh, look. There's Dino and Milly over by the doggie daycare area. Maybe they've heard something. Let's go talk to them. It's worth a shot." Jaz led the way over to the dog pen before I had a chance to voice my concerns.

I pushed my apprehensions aside and followed her.

"Jaz, I'm so sorry. I feel horrible about what happened. I should have been there." Milly wrung her hands together over her baby bump. The petite redhead's pale green eyes were filled with worry and regret.

Dino pushed his glasses up, then rubbed a hand over his wild auburn curls before awkwardly patting her back. "It's not your fault."

"Dino's right, Milly," Jaz said. "I'm so relieved you weren't there. I would never forgive myself if something bad happened to you."

"I put up a flyer about the missing puppies at my daycare," Dino said to Jaz. "I'll let you know if I hear anything."

"I appreciate that, Dino." Jaz shot him a grateful

smile.

Dino nodded once, then his gaze drifted across the park over by the gazebo where Hannah Schwartz was doing her stand-up act. "Excuse me, ladies. I think I'll take my break now if you're okay on your own, Milly."

"Absolutely." Milly tilted her head. "And thanks, Dino."

He nodded once and made a beeline for the gazebo.

"He must really like stand-up comedy," Jaz said.

"More like Raven Monroe." Milly pointed to a woman in the audience.

"It *is* spring," I said, "and as the mamas would say, he definitely has the fever." That was the same woman I saw him talking to the other day with the black and brown highlighted hair, leather jacket, and metal choker necklace.

"I like her style." Jaz studied the woman. "Who is she?"

"I just met her the other day at Dino's Daycare," Milly said. "Dino is a smitten kitten. It's so cute how flustered he gets around her. I'm happy he's finally found someone. We dated once years ago when I first started working for him, but we both decided we were better off as friends. Then I met and married Nelson, and well, the rest is history." Milly patted her belly with a smile. "Speaking of weddings, how is the planning coming along?"

"At a snail's pace." Jaz sighed. "I can't even imagine a future without Chanel and Versace in it. I still can't believe no one has reported any tips. The sheer number of puppies, amount of food, and noise that goes along with all that had to have turned up a few clues. Yet no one has come forward with anything."

"We'll find them." I nodded with determination. "I

have faith." Another rumble of thunder sounded a little closer this time.

A few dogs in the dog park howled their fear of the thunder.

"That's my cue. I agree with Kalli. Don't lose hope, Jaz," Milly said, then hurried away to tend to the whining dogs.

"I'm trying not to," Jaz said at her retreating back then glanced up at the sky with a frown before looking back at me and changing the subject. "I appreciate you letting us live with you temporarily, but now my snail's pace at wedding planning has become your snail's pace at finishing your remodel. I'm bad luck."

"You're not bad luck, and you're not the reason for the pause," I quickly pointed out, adjusting my backpack.

My fears and insecurities had always been the reason for any stalls Nik and I had in taking our relationship to the next level. That and the string of murders occurring in Clearview over the past year. If anyone was bad luck, it appeared to be me.

"Well, my situation certainly hasn't helped." Jaz rubbed her arms.

"It's not just your situation." I frowned, rubbing my own. The temperature had dropped several degrees. "Nik and Boomer have never been busier. Murder, puppy-napping, counterfeit money. I feel like there has to have been a full moon or something, because my Aunt Tasoula isn't the only one who's gone crazy."

"Boomer said Nelson had a counterfeit twenty-dollar bill just yesterday at the jewelry store," Jaz interjected. "He said with so many outsiders in town, it was hard to tell where it might have come from at this point, or if it's the last of its kind. And not enough people know how to check if a bill is counterfeit."

I glanced over at Milly. "That has to be stressful on Milly in her condition, yet she stays so calm."

"She really is a dog whisperer. Look how she's managed to calm the entire pack down." Lightning streaked across the sky way off in the distance. "I bet they close the festival down with that storm coming."

Just then an announcement sounded across the speakers for folks to wrap things up. Big fat raindrops started to fall.

"Just great. We didn't bring any umbrellas." I slipped the hood on my jacket up over my hair.

"Well, all I know is I, for one, can't take any more drama." Jaz scooped her hair into a messy bun. "Let's go."

So much for distracting her.

Just then a loud commotion happened over at the gazebo, and someone screamed. Jaz and I ran over to investigate as the sky opened up and started pouring rain. Even through the deluge of rain, there was no mistaking Hannah Schwartz passed out in a heap on the gazebo floor with something falling out of her pocket.

I bent down to look at the bottle and then glanced up at Jaz. "When Doc called with your test results, what kind of drug did he say was in your system?"

"It was a benzodiazepine, why?"

"Bingo." I pointed to the bottle on the ground.

The same sedative someone had used to drug Jaz lay beside Hannah.

～

THAT EVENING, Nik and Boomer walked through the front door of his half of our house, looking exhausted. Once they cleared the doorway and spent ten minutes pacifying Wolfgang as he showered them with slob-bery hugs and kisses, they walked through the opening in the wall and joined Jaz and me at my kitchen table for dinner.

Earlier, Jaz and I had left the festival and gone to the hospital, but they wouldn't give us any news about Hannah because we weren't family or the police. I had questions. Was Hannah the one drugging people? Or did someone drug her and drop the vial? So, I had called Nik to let him know what had happened. I real-ized I'd forgotten my backpack at the park. Jaz and I went back for it, and thankfully, it was still there. Then we headed home to dry out and wait for news after getting thoroughly soaked in the rain.

"That smells amazing." Nik washed his hands in the sink for two full minutes, then kissed the top of my head before taking a seat at the table.

"Thank you. I'm trying to broaden my culinary skills. You can thank your ma for this recipe." I'd made Keftedes, which were Greek meatballs, and one of Nik's favorites. I was trying to do something nice for him since I'd kind of messed up our plans lately. Judging by the look on his face, I'd succeeded.

Nik made the sign of the cross and sent a prayer up to the gods.

We all laughed.

Boomer started to sit, but Jaz pointed to the sink. He shot a quick apologetic look at me, and I sent him a reassuring smile back, as he hurried to wash his hands before taking the seat at the table beside her. I was sure they were ready to find a house of their own. It wasn't easy living with people after having your own place, but living with quirky people could be espe-cially difficult.

That was why I adored Nik all the more.

Wolfgang followed the aromas, but he took one look at me and sprawled out on the floor beside my feet. I blew him a kiss full of promise that I would pet him after dinner, of course. Prissy waltzed into the room, turned her nose up at him, then gave me a disappointed look before perching on the windowsill. Jaz poured some chardonnay for me and her, then opened two longneck beers for the guys. We took a few minutes to savor dinner before jumping into conversation.

"This is delicious, Kalli. Thank you," Boomer said.

"You're very welcome, Boomer. I try." My chest filled with warmth and pride. It was nice to feel *that* rather than wariness and panic for a change.

"And you succeed," Nik added, rubbing his belly.

"Much better than I can do," Jaz said.

"Babe, you succeed in other ways." Boomer winked.

Jaz laughed and shook her head. "Anyway, did you two find out anything at the hospital?"

"Apparently, Hannah has a prescription for the same sedative used to drug Jaz. She still gets anxious when performing her stand-up comedy on stage, so she uses the sedative in low doses to help relax her."

"That didn't look like a low dose to me," Jaz said. "She literally passed out in the middle of performing."

"She claims she took the normal amount," Boomer said, "but Doc LaLone confirmed there was more than that in her system."

"So, either she was lying about how much she took...or someone laced her drink with more as well." I looked at Nik. "But why?"

"Good question." Nik checked his notes.

"Maybe she knows something about the puppy-napping, and someone is trying to silence her?" Boomer speculated.

"She did tell me how adorable the puppies were, and how she always wanted a dog," Jaz said. "I told her there were still some available, but she said she was on tour, and it wouldn't be fair to drag a puppy with her."

"I just remembered something." I looked at Nik and Boomer. "I didn't think anything of it at the time, but when I was at Stallone's Supermarket, I had Wolfgang's dogfood on my list, but they were sold out. I checked the pet store and the vet, but they were sold out as well. I had to buy it online."

"Chanel and Versace eat the same dog food," Boomer pointed out.

"The puppies are still nursing, but if someone knew they were going to steal them, then they would also know they had to feed their mamas," Nik added. "Was their dog food missing when they were taken?"

Boomer nodded.

Nik looked at me. "You might be onto something, Ballas."

"I hope so." I was getting worried we were running out of time.

"If we find out who bought up all the dogfood, we just might find our thief," Boomer agreed. "I'll check into that first thing in the morning."

"Can't we look into it now?" Jaz wrung her hands together.

"No place is open tonight, babe." Boomer pulled her onto his lap and hugged her. "The dogs will be okay. They're too young to sell just yet, and they're worth too much to harm them. We'll find them."

"How can you be so sure?" She sniffled.

He stroked her back. "Because I won't stop looking until we do."

8

———

"**H**i, Maria, we'll have the usual," Jaz said as we stepped up to the counter of Sinfully Delicious the next morning to place our coffee and pastry orders. The earthy aromas of tea and coffee beans along with the sweet smells of cinnamon and sugar filled the air. "How are the wedding plans coming along?"

"Right on schedule for this summer. Sully and I are so excited." Maria beamed, her round rosy cheeks glowing. "I'll be placing an order for my wedding night trousseau soon, Kalli. I just can't figure out what I want exactly."

"Don't you worry about that. I have some ideas." I winked at her.

One of my greatest joys was helping women to feel confident. Zeus only knew how Jaz and the women in my crazy family had helped me grow. It was important for women to uplift one another and be there for each other. I never would have been able to come this far without them.

"Yay!" She clapped her hands, tucked her dark hair beneath her hairnet, and then looked back at Jaz. "How about you guys? Are you and Detective Matheson all set for your big day? You're getting married next summer, too, right?"

"Right, but we're not even close to being ready." Jaz sighed. "It's hard for me to get excited or make plans with the puppies missing."

Maria's excited expression transformed into one of sympathy. "I heard. I'm so sorry. I can't imagine what you're going through with your girls missing, and those poor babies. You must be distraught." She reached across the counter and handed Jaz a bag of goodies. "I gave you a little something extra to cheer you up."

"Thanks, Maria. It hasn't been easy, but people like Kalli and you make it bearable." Jaz smiled. "You're a good friend."

"It's the least I can do." Maria looked at me. "How's the murder investigation coming along? I can't imagine what you're going through, either, with your poor aunt being a suspect. She must be a nervous wreck."

"One would think." Logically, most normal people would be a mess, but not Aunt Tasoula. "My aunt has a way of always seeing the positive side of things." She was in denial, not accepting that prison might be a real possibility if we couldn't find a way to clear her name. My aunt might be crazy, but she wasn't a killer.

"My bakery is my life. I don't know what I would do if someone was murdered here?" Maria shuddered, continuing to work without missing a beat. "Whatever is she doing to stay busy with her salon being temporarily closed?"

"Majoretting," I said dryly.

Maria's face scrunched up. "What on earth does that mean?"

"Like the TV show The Bachelorette. It involves

baton ceremonies, group dates, and one-on-ones. She's already home so *all* her dates are hometowns, but I seriously hope she draws the line at the fantasy suite." That was an image I suddenly couldn't get out of my head.

Maria arched her brows high. "I still don't really understand."

"Trust me," Jaz replied. "You don't want to know any more details."

Maria shrugged. "Well, you ladies have a great day." She motioned the next person forward and took their order.

Jaz and I headed for the front door when I spotted Chelsea and Grant at a table in the corner. I paused and Jaz followed my gaze. Her eyes grew wide with stars in them. She made a beeline for their table.

"Grant Kingsley, as I live and breathe, it's a pleasure to meet you." Jaz held out her hand and practically swooned.

A flash of irritation crossed Grant's face until he got a good look at Jaz. He might be a movie star, but he was still a man. "The pleasure is all mine, darlin'." He kissed her hand. "And you are...?"

A trill of a giggle slipped out of her mouth. "Jazlyn Alvarez, but you can call me Jaz. Everyone does."

"Including her fiancé," I said, and then whispered in her ear as I grabbed her arm. "Since when do you have a southern accent?"

She peeked back at me with a half-smile. *Since he starred in Indiana Bones and the Temple of the South.*

I dropped her arm and tried hard not to roll my eyes.

"It's nice to see you again, Ms. Turner." I smiled at Chelsea.

Her remarkable lavender eyes were currently filled with impatience. She nodded once, then looked away.

My gaze landed on Grant. "I don't think we've met yet. I'm Kalli Ballas. Tasoula Ballas is my aunt." I held out my hand.

Grant shook my hand, his striking features softening into an expression of genuine sympathy. "Ah, Leon Cajones widow. He was a good man. Always nice to me before my *glow up* as the kids say. I was sorry to hear he passed." His hand still lingered in my grip. *I see Tasoula changed her name back. She always was a firecracker. Still is, by the look of it. I wonder if she's single. I would have found out if annoying Skylar hadn't interfered as usual. She got what was coming to her...and so did I.*

I dropped my hand and rubbed my palm on my skirt, suddenly feeling the need for a shower. "What did you get?"

Grant's face puckered with a flash of alarm and then confusion as he gave me a wary look. "Excuse me?"

Shoot. I had a bad habit of speaking my thoughts out loud. "Uh, what did you get for breakfast?"

He glanced down at the bare space in front of him with only a mug sitting there. "Coffee. I don't eat breakfast. Never have."

"You should. It's the most important meal of the day, you know." I tended to ramble when I got nervous. "Statistics show people who break their fast by eating breakfast have more energy, think clearer, and live longer."

"I'll take my chances." He studied me curiously. "You don't look anything like your aunt or your mother."

I shrugged and repeated for the millionth time in

my life, "I'm adopted, but don't tell Ma. I think she's forgotten she never gave birth to me." I winked.

He laughed.

"Can we help you with something, Ms. Ballas?" Chelsea glanced at her watch.

"Oh, I'm sorry. I didn't mean to interrupt."

"Chelsea and I go way back," Grant interjected. "She's a flight attendant. Sometimes I see her on my travels. We were just catching up about a new movie I'm going to be filming out west this summer."

"*The Lonesome Cowboy.* I saw the announcement." Jaz squealed, hopping up and down and clapping her hands. "It sounds fabulous."

I arched an eyebrow high.

"Maybe you should come to the premier," he said smoothly.

"She should?" Chelsea tucked her silver strands behind her ears, leveling lavender eyes on him.

"She can't." I was already shaking my head.

"I can't?" Jaz blinked, still in a star-struck daze.

"She'll be getting married to Boomer Matheson. He's a detective." I looked Grant in the eye. "Maybe you've heard of him?"

Grant's eyes narrowed on me as if just now remembering I was still there as he muttered, "You're definitely not like your aunt."

"I can assure you, I'm not." I held his gaze, refusing to back down.

"We have to go." Chelsea stood.

"Of course." I took a step back as I looked at Grant again. "I wouldn't want to keep you from your family."

A muscle in his jaw bulged as he stood and gave us a slight bow. "Ms. Ballas. Ms. Alvarez. Good day, ladies." And then he waltzed out of the bakery with his head held high as if he were walking the red carpet.

"Wasn't he dreamy?" The words purred out of Jaz's mouth.

"He was something," I replied, my gut telling me he was *up* to something for sure. And I was determined to find out what.

~

ON MY LUNCH break at Full Disclosure, I grabbed my backpack and decided to step outside for some fresh air. My mind was not in a creative mode to design my summer line of lingerie. I couldn't focus on that any more than I could focus on the remodel.

I couldn't do anything until my aunt's name was cleared and this murder was solved.

I got in my car and started to drive, and before I knew it, I ended up at the Clearview Motel. It was a two-story motel that had just been renovated. Ever since Larry Miller hired Gary Bolin to run it, business was booming. Gary used to be the town drunk and had fancied me, but after he cleaned up his act and met Maria's bookkeeper, Lisa Chamberlain, he'd become a respectable citizen and a good friend.

In the parking lot, I was once again struck with the sensation of being watched. I tightened my hand on my pack and quickly wandered inside the motel, looking over my shoulder every step of the way. The last thing I wanted was to be caught unaware.

Bouncing off the person in front of me, I whipped my head back around. "I'm so sorry," I said to the man with blond hair from my aunt's salon.

"No worries." The man adjusted his lopsided spectacles and flashed his dimples at me before letting me pass, then he headed out the door with a newspaper tucked beneath his arm and a purpose to his strides.

"Who was that?" I asked Gary as I walked up to the front desk. It was so hard to keep up with the out-of-towners.

Gary raised his kind, green eyes and welcomed me with a warm smile, his waves of dirty blond hair accentuating his Hollywood heartthrob face. Love obviously agreed with him. "Nolan Ryder," he answered my question as he looked out the door to the parking lot. "He's in town for the spring festival."

"Alone?" I was always surprised and a little envious at how brave and independent people could be.

"Apparently so." Gary shrugged as if it was no big deal.

"I admire people who aren't afraid to venture out on their own. I don't know if I could do that."

"I used to travel alone all the time before I met Lisa. Solitude was kind of nice sometimes, but there's something comforting about knowing another person is by your side to share life with."

I thought of Nik and felt grateful. Gary was right. "How's Lisa?"

"Better than ever." He grinned. "How's Nik?"

"Busier than ever." I sighed.

"I heard. A lot of crazy things happening around town lately." He ran a hand through his wavy hair. "Give your aunt and ma my best."

"I will. Ma has some Baklava for you. It's being made, and I'll bring it by soon." Just as soon as I told Ma I promised him some.

His eyes sprang wide, and he rubbed his hands together on a moan. "I'm not about to argue with that, but what's the occasion?"

"You know Ma. If she likes you, she doesn't need

an occasion." That part was true at least. I did my best impersonation of Ma. "A man's gotta eat, okay? Okay."

"Well, okay." He rubbed his stomach.

We both laughed.

"How can I help you, Kalli?"

"Do you know anything about Grant Kingsley?"

"On the record, I don't have a Grant Kingsley staying here." Gary looked around, but the lobby was empty. "Off the record, he uses an alias. His wife, kids, and nanny are here every day, but he rarely is."

"Where does he go?"

"She says he's visiting his old hangout spots from high school and catching up with old friends." Gary shrugged. "He's got a great looking family. If they were mine, I would be parading them around town and showing them off to my friends, not hiding them away from everyone."

"Me too. I wonder why he doesn't?"

"Apparently, he's trying to keep them *safe*."

"I get that. I mean, there is still a murderer out there. You would think Grant would fear for his own safety as well, but that doesn't stop him from going out. Unless he has nothing to fear because he is in fact the murderer." I blinked. I really had to stop saying everything that popped into my head out loud.

"Who is?" a familiar deep voice said from behind me.

I jumped, then took a deep breath and slowly turned around. "Gary here." I pointed to the hotel manager. "Didn't you know he is the murderer of dessert?" I smiled, showing all my teeth. "I stopped by to tell him Ma has some Baklava for him."

Gary's eyebrows shot up as he looked back and forth between the two of us. I didn't have to read his mind to know he was silently pleading the fifth. The phone rang, and he yanked the receiver to his ear, looking relieved.

"Right." Nik grunted, looking away from Gary and back to me. "You came out of your way when you could have just called." He stood with his sport coat parted and his hands on his jean clad hips.

"I'm blocked creatively, so I went for a drive." I frowned and crossed my arms. "Why are you here?"

"I'm here checking on the same thing I imagine you are." He leveled a knowing look at me with his sizzling sapphire eyes. "A certain celebrity who's staying at this hotel yet never seems to be around."

The elevator dinged and Clayton Brown stepped into the lobby.

Saved by the bell. I let out a relieved breath.

Nik gave me a knowing smirk.

"Detective Stevens, it's nice to see you again." Clayton came to a stop beside us and held out his hand.

Nik smiled wide and shook the older man's hand. "Great game this morning. You have quite the handicap."

"Game?" I asked, looking between the two men. Now it was my turn to be suspicious. Who had time to play games? Was no one but me worried about my aunt going away for murder?

"My buddy works at the golf course, and this unseasonably warm spring weather allowed for him to open early during the festival. Your pop, papou, myself, and Clayton here played nine holes."

Golf? My jaw fell open. "Aren't you supposed to be investigating a murder and clearing Aunt Tasoula's name?"

"Ah, you must be Kalli. Your aunt has told me so much about you." Clayton smiled at me with an unusual shade of brown eyes. He was a handsome man. I could see why my aunt was drawn to him, even though he was vastly different from Tate. "The golf was for charity, my dear. Your aunt is the one who set it up." He stood a little straighter and beamed. "I won the date with the family, apparently, while the other suiters won a group date with each other."

I rubbed my throbbing temples. Clearly, everyone had gone crazy. "Where was my aunt? Isn't she supposed to be present at both?" I asked. Who knew what rules my aunt put in place. The majorette was uncharted territory.

Clayton's brow puckered, his dark mustache and hair not moving an inch. "I'm still unclear how this whole majorette thing works, but as long as I get a baton during the ceremony, I'm not questioning anything." His gaze softened and he chuckled. "You're aunt's an interesting woman."

"With a boyfriend," I muttered, then startled when I realized I'd said that out loud and they had both heard me.

"They're on a break," Clayton and Nik replied at the same time.

I threw up my hands on a huff and decided living in the twilight zone wasn't helping my creative block, either. I couldn't keep up with my aunt, and if she wasn't going to take her being the prime suspect seriously, then why should I?

"You win. I give up. I'll see you at home," I said to Nik. "Nice to finally meet you, Clayton." Then I spun on my heel and left the motel.

I reached my car and was about to get in when I saw my aunt pull into the parking lot. I couldn't believe my eyes. She wore big sunglasses and a hat, but I would recognize her anywhere. She pulled up to the curb and out climbed the French brothers, Antione and Louis Dupont. She blew them a kiss and then she peeled out, rounding the corner on two wheels.

They waved until she disappeared. I started walking toward them, but they didn't go into the hotel. They got into their car and headed off somewhere quickly, as if in a hurry. Whatever that meant.

And the Twilight Zone continued.

9

———

"Almost done," I said to Maria as I took the last of her measurements that afternoon up in my loft at Full Disclosure.

I'd gone back to work after my lunch break, marveling over how I could have left my backpack unzipped. I never did that before and didn't remember doing so now. It just went to show how frazzled I was lately. I tried to focus on things I could control. Like designing Maria's wedding trousseau.

The store was buzzing with customers, and Jaz had been busy all day. Everyone had spring fever, and love was in the air. Not to mention, Jaz's spring finds were fresh and new and flying off the shelves.

"I just love all four of the ideas you came up with." Maria lowered her arms to her sides now that I was finished.

"Oh, I'm so glad." I wrote the last of her measurements in my book. "What one do you like the best?"

"All of them." She sighed. "I like all of them. How am I supposed to decide what one to wear on my wedding night?"

"Who says you have to decide?" Jaz poked her

head into my loft from the top of the stairs. She cleaned her hands with the hand sanitizer I had by the railing. "May I come in?" She looked in question at us both since this was Maria's consultation.

I looked at Maria who nodded her consent. "Yes, of course," I said. The loft was technically Jaz's, but I did rent it, and Jaz had always been respectful of my space and my time.

"Oh, I can't possibly take them all." Maria bit her lip as she flipped through my sketchbook, her eyes filled with excitement. She looked at me. "Can I?"

"I don't see why not. You're the bride, and this is your wedding night. You can do whatever you want. I'm just glad you like the designs. I hope they make you feel special because you are."

"These are perfect. I appreciate you using realistic lifelike mannequins." Maria was a curvy full-figured woman. She studied the mannequin I had draped with fabric pinned together in a mockup of one of the negligees I could sew, and her eyes filled with shimmering excitement. "I can already see I will look like a goddess in these."

"Because you are one." Jaz stepped over to join Maria in studying the mannequin with appreciation.

I smiled, feeling happy. This was the part of my job that I loved the most. Seeing a woman's face light up and knowing I had helped her feel beautiful in her own skin. I recognized the importance of using mannequins in all shapes and sizes. Women needed to see themselves represented, and it helped me in designing flattering pieces for everyone.

"These really are stunning, Kalli." Jaz flipped through the pages of my sketchbook. "Some of your best work yet."

"Thank you. Must be the mamas are rubbing off on me. There's just something about the spring that inspires love."

"I can't wait to see what Kalli comes up with for *your* trousseau, Jaz." Maria gathered her things, preparing to leave.

"If the wedding even happens." Jaz put on a smile as a front, but I knew she was still sad and worried sick on the inside. "I just don't see how I can still get married in the summer at this rate."

"Keep the faith, my friend." Maria patted her arm. "I'm sure they'll turn up soon. Twenty-two puppies and two big dogs are a lot for anyone to hide."

"I sure hope you're right." Jaz squeezed her hand. "Thanks, Maria. Save me one of your sinfully delicious cinnamon rolls, and I'll stop over after work."

"You got it." Maria's gaze landed on me. "Thanks again, Kalli. You really did an outstanding job. I feel beautiful."

"My pleasure," I said and meant it. "I'll let you know when all four designs are finished and ready for a fitting."

"Sounds perfect." Maria waved as she left the loft.

I joined Jaz by the railing, overlooking the store below. "You're going to need more inventory."

"Isn't it crazy that not too long ago Ana and I were fighting over customers," Jaz said with wonder, "now neither of us can keep enough inventory in stock."

"'Tis the season." I lifted my hands.

Anastatia Stewert owned Vixens, the main competitor for Full Disclosure. She and Jaz used to be at odds with each other, but ever since Nik's ma came to Clearview and several of her family members like Thalia had flocked after her, we had twice the number of Greeks in town who loved to shop. That meant more than enough customers for both of them.

"Hey, I wanted to thank you again for letting Boomer and me crash at your place. I know it's not convenient, but I just can't handle seeing that empty puppy room." Jaz's voice cracked, revealing her vulnerability.

"You know you're always welcome." I infused mine with tenderness. "And technically the house still belongs to you. Nik and I are just renting."

"For now," she replied with honesty. "I wouldn't have let you two remodel unless I thought you were serious about buying the place."

My stomach flipped. "Serious about moving in together, yes, but that's about all I can handle at the moment."

"Touché" Jaz let me off the hook, distracted by something. She squinted, leaning forward to look down into the store below. "Hey, isn't that Milly?"

I followed her gaze and watched Milly look around the room and then walk over to a woman. "Yes, and that looks like Raven with her."

Jaz scanned her shop. "I don't see Dino."

Raven's hands started moving faster as she talked. Suddenly, she spun on her heel and stormed out the door.

Milly wrung her hands, appearing upset.

"Well, that doesn't look good," I said.

"Milly is Dino's best friend. Maybe he's having problems with Raven, and she's trying to fix it."

"Or maybe *she* is the problem."

"Only one way to find out." Jaz led the way downstairs. We didn't stop walking until we caught Milly before she could escape out the door.

"Milly, are you okay?" I asked.

Her hands dropped to her stomach, and she inhaled a slow, deep breath. "I'm fine. It's just been a long day."

"I hear that." Jaz flipped her hair over one shoulder, studying Milly. "I saw you talking to Raven. She looked angry. Is something wrong?"

Milly hesitated. "No, everything is fine. We just had a little misunderstanding." She glanced at her watch. "Well, look at the time. I have to go relieve Dino at the daycare. You ladies take care." She hurried outside, but she didn't head to her car. She met up with a woman I had never seen.

"Who's that?" I asked, pointing to the street just as Milly got in the woman's car and they drove off together.

"I don't know. I've never seen her before, but I can tell you one thing. I know Milly, and she is definitely not fine."

"THALIA HAS a house for us to look at that she thinks will be perfect," Boomer said to Jaz the second we got home.

"Oh my gosh, really?" Jaz's face lit up.

She had lived with me in this house for years, but I knew she missed living alone with Boomer in his apartment. Of course, I also knew she couldn't wait to find that perfect place to call their own that would feel like both of theirs.

Their forever home.

"Yes, really. And she's waiting for us there right now." Boomer's eyes twinkled with barely contained excitement. "The seller is planning an open house, but Thalia managed to score us a sneak peek."

"What about dinner?" She looked at me with an apologetic expression as I held the steaming take-out Mexican food we'd picked up from Rosalita's restaurant. "I hate to skip out on Kalli and Nik after they've been so good to us."

"Don't worry about us." I handed the take-out food to Nik. "I'm crossing my fingers that this house is *the one* for you guys."

"Thanks, Kalli." Jaz beamed.

"Of course." I smiled.

"Come on." Boomer took Jaz's hand. "We'll grab dinner when we're done. We don't want to keep Thalia waiting."

"Okay." Jaz hurried out the door without a single glance back.

I joined Nik at the table. He already had a glass of chardonnay for me and a beer for him. "What's that?" I pointed to a gawdy statue in the corner of the kitchen with a Marti bracelet slipped over its wrist.

"Don't worry, it's not permanent. The mamas somehow got in and sprinkled around their idea of décor in their attempt to *help* us."

I rolled my eyes. "We need to change the locks."

"They don't have a key."

"Then how...never mind. I don't even want to know. On a more positive note, I'm thrilled for Jaz and Boomer. I really hope they find their dream house. She's been so sad since the puppies went missing."

Wolfgang's ears perked up, and he whined. I felt the same way when I thought of those poor, helpless babies, especially the smallest one with the droopy weeping willow eyes.

"Boomer, too." Nik gave the large Saint Bernard a scratch on the top of his massive block of a head. "It's okay, buddy." Wolf laid down beside Prissy, and she didn't move or hiss. Progress. Then Nik squirted hand sanitizer into his hands and winked at me before filling his plate with food.

The man knew me so well.

"Have you had any leads on the puppy-nappers?" I took a bite of fish tacos and tried not to moan in pleasure.

The grilled tilapia with red cabbage, onion, avocado, tomato, lettuce, cotija cheese, and a lime garlic cream sauce made with Rosalita's not-so-secret ingredient, Sriracha. created a perfect combination of flavors that danced over my tastebuds.

Nik chuckled softly, watching me until my question registered. His smile slipped, and he sighed, running a hand over the back of his neck and rolling his head. "We followed up on where all the dogfood went. The trail of kibble lead to Clearview Campgrounds."

I sucked in a breath, feeling a spark of hope. "Isn't that where Malik and Keisha Cooper are staying in that big camper?"

"Bingo."

"Why would they buy up so much dog food?" I voiced my suspicions, praying I was right.

"That was my question exactly, so I followed up." Nik took a swig of his longneck beer then set it on the table. He looked tired.

"Please tell me you found Channel and Versace?"

He was already shaking his head. "I was hopeful about that as well, but no. It turns out the Coopers have several purebred golden retrievers that they show in dog show competitions all over the place. That's why they drove their camper to Clearview Campgrounds instead of staying in the motel. They were supposed to go to a dog show in Massachusetts after the reunion, but they missed it because they aren't cleared to leave town yet. Let's just say they weren't too happy about that."

"That doesn't mean they couldn't have stolen the poodles." I sipped my chardonnay, pondering this idea. "Maybe they're hiding them someplace else. The poodles are purebreds and gorgeous. I bet they would do well in a dog show ring."

"True, but then where are the puppies?" Nik lifted his hands. "Saint Berdoodles are a popular mixed breed as pets, but mixed breeds typically aren't connected to the dog show ring. Dog show rings focus on one type of purebred for each category, no mixes."

"Okay, well, here's another thought." My mind was spinning with ideas. "The dog show ring can be expensive. Maybe they stole the puppies to sell off to help fund their dog competitions."

"Maybe." Nik nodded. "Connecticut is a small state with a high population density, but there is still enough rural land with remote cabins scattered around. I'll get someone on it to talk to the forest rangers." He pinched the bridge of his nose as if he had a headache then looked at me without as much hope as I'd like. "It's worth a shot because no other leads have turned up in town."

"I'm starting to get worried the puppies and their mamas are gone forever." As much as I freaked out over the thought of twenty-two fur babies, I never realized how much I would miss them once they were gone. I couldn't imagine what they were going through.

"You and me both, but we can't give up hope." He

picked up our plates after we were finished and threw them in the trash.

"Speaking of getting worried. What about Skylar's murder?" I finished the rest of my chardonnay. "Any new leads there?"

"You were right. There's definitely something going on with Ursula and Drake. I tailed him and he had lunch at Vincenzo Ricci's restaurant. Vincenzo came out and sat at his table for a while talking. I spoke with Vinny after Drake was gone, and he said they were friends back in high school, but Vinny is a year older and was in your aunt's grade."

"What did Drake want?"

Nik shrugged. "Vinny was tight-lipped. Just said they were catching up, but I got the feeling there was more to it than that."

"How does Ursula come into play?" I tilted my head and waited.

Nikos the Greek paused in dramatic fashion before dropping the bomb in true Greek fashion. "When Drake left, I tailed him. He ended up at the lookout. Guess who showed up and got in his car for an hour?"

"Ursula?" My eyebrows shot up.

"One and the same."

I blinked. "But last I saw them together, they were arguing and acted like they hated each other."

Nik shook his head. "From my viewpoint, they had their heads bent close together and looked pretty chummy."

"Was her girlfriend with her?"

"No. And when I followed up with her, she was *not* happy to hear that Ursula had been spending time with Drake. They used to date back in the day, I guess."

"Interesting. Trouble in paradise?" I got up and

carried my wine glass to the sink, ready to put this day behind me.

"Maybe." He accidentally knocked my backpack purse to the floor and a twenty fell out. "Whoops." He bent down and picked up the money, and then frowned.

"What's wrong?"

"I'm not sure. Hang on." He inspected the bill carefully and then held it up to the light. "Just as I thought."

"What?"

"Feel this paper." He handed me the bill.

I felt it. "It feels smooth."

"Exactly. Genuine currency is printed on special paper with a unique texture that feels slightly rough. And when you hold this bill up to the light, the watermark is poorly reproduced compared to genuine bills." He grabbed his wallet off the counter and pulled out a twenty then held it up beside my twenty so I could see the difference.

"The bill you had is also missing the security thread that runs through the bill. There's no micro-printing on this one because the tiny text is difficult to reproduce. I'm sure if I held this under ultraviolet light, this bill wouldn't react correctly. The size and thickness of this bill doesn't match the standard bill precisely. I have to follow up to be sure. Another way of checking if a bill is counterfeit is to use a security pen. We have some at the station. If a security pen is used on this bill, it will most likely turn blue."

"How so?" I was genuinely curious as I loved re-searching random facts.

Nik was loving every minute of this because he knew something I didn't. "Because," he dragged out his explanation, "genuine currency doesn't react to iodine, but counterfeit notes turn dark blue when exposed because of starch in the paper."

I stared at the bills in fascination. "I had no idea so much went into producing counterfeit money."

"It's an intricate process to be sure. The United States goes to great lengths to put safety measures in place, but counterfeiters are getting more sophisticated, which is why all these counterfeit bills showing up in one place is confusing."

I looked up at him. "How come?"

"Counterfeiters are smart. They distribute their bills without raising suspicion by passing the fake money through various channels like exchanging them for genuine money or buying goods and services. But they avoid detection by operating covertly, changing locations often, and using multiple identities. That makes it surprising that so many bills are showing up in one place like Clearview."

"With so many people in town, who knows how many hands this twenty passed through before it got me." The very thought made me want to go wash my hands. "I got it from Rosalita's when I picked up our take-out dinner tonight."

"I'll talk with Rosalita tomorrow morning." Nik made a note in his notebook.

"What can I do?"

His demeanor turned serious. "Nothing, remember? I know it's hard, Ballas, but I don't want you involved."

"But the counterfeit money and the puppy-napping don't have anything to do with the murder investigation, so why can't I help?"

"Because it's dangerous, Kalli," he said softly.

Using my first name meant he was concerned. "I don't know what I would do if anything happened to you."

Well, how could I argue with those pleading sapphire blue eyes? Simple. I wouldn't *argue*...but that didn't mean I would sit back and do nothing.

I had a few ideas of my own.

10

"So, did you like the house?" I asked Jaz the next morning at Full Disclosure. She and Boomer got back so late; I had already gone to bed. And this morning, Jaz left for work before I got up.

She hopped up and down. "Yes, oh my lord, it's everything we both want. It's four bedrooms, two and a half baths, a finished basement, and a fenced in yard. Big enough for a growing family, and the dogs."

"I'm so happy for you." I gave her a hug.

She didn't look sad anymore. She looked determined. "We *will* get my dogs back. I'm confident because the alternative is unthinkable."

"Good." I nodded once. "The power of positive thinking is real. No negative juju in the universe."

"Amen, sister. Just like I'm determined to get married this summer as well, so I've got lots to do. No time to wallow in self-pity anymore. And that starts with packing up Boomer's apartment, so feel free to proceed with your remodel. We're moving back home until we close on the new house."

"Are you sure?" I frowned. "I don't want you to think you're unwelcome to stay with Nik and me." And

I wasn't ready to be alone and have that talk about our future with Nik just yet.

"I know I'm welcome, and I thank you and Nik for that. Boomer and I really appreciate everything you've done for us, but it's time to go home."

"Well, let me know if you need any help packing."

"Careful." She laughed. "I just might take you up on that."

My cell phone rang as customers came into the store, so I stepped away to answer while Jaz waited on them.

"Milly, is everything okay?" She was walking Wolfgang and then dropping him off at Dino's Daycare like she did several times a week while Nik and I were at work. There had never been an issue with him before.

"Well, I'm not sure. He seems really distracted today, and I keep finding kibble in the most random places outside. It's like he's a blood hound. He's on the scent of something. I love walking him, but his pulling today is a bit much for me this late in my pregnancy."

Oh, no. That couldn't be good. "Where are you? I'll come get him immediately so stay put."

"I brought him into our jewelry store to distract him from whatever has him so engaged. He's a big hit with the customers."

"I'll be right there." I hung up and sent Jaz a text that I had to step out for a bit. Then I headed down the street to Rockwell Jewelers.

It was right down the road and didn't take me long to get there.

Walking inside, I was surprised to see Antoine and Louis Dupont, looking at colorful Greek jewelry. Nelson Rockwell was a smart man. Between the Ballas and Pagonis families, it was a good idea to keep a whole section of the store that catered to them.

The men were admiring vibrant gemstones like turquoise, amethyst, coral, and lapis lazuli. These gems were commonly used by the Greeks as focal points in rings, necklaces, and bracelets. There was only one reason the brothers would be interested in jewelry like this.

Aunt Tasoula.

It wasn't like my aunt was a twin, and Ma was married. What good could possibly come from *both* the men pursuing her? Maybe they thought she would be willing to let them share her and date them both. I knew my aunt still had feelings for Tate. She was just angry and hurt that he was giving her a taste of her own medicine.

That was the whole reason behind her being *The Majorette*.

The Dupont brothers' eyes lit up when they saw me.

"Kalli Ballas, oui?" Antoine said with a thick French accent, his black hair slicked back with only a hint of gray at the temples.

"That's right." I smiled and shook his hand.

He smiled wide, but it didn't quite reach his dark eyes. *Hmmm, I need to get the family on my side if I'm going to win the final baton, but this one is smart. She might be harder to crack than the rest.* "I'm Antoine. It's lovely to finally meet you."

Lovely? He'd just insulted my family. There wasn't anything *lovely* about him. I knew his kind. I just hoped he wasn't playing games with my aunt's emotions. "Likewise," I finally replied. I had to fight to keep my smile in place as I pulled my hand away and looked at his brother. "You must be Louis. My aunt has told me all about you both."

Louis kept his smile pasted on his face, showing

all his teeth as he took my hand and kissed the back of my fingers, sending my germ radar into overdrive. *I'll have to watch what I say with this one. She could influence Tasoula's decision.* "I hope it was all good. And it's a pleasure to meet someone as beautiful as your aunt."

I nodded, slipping my hand out of his as soon as possible without appearing rude.

His hair was also dark but parted on the side instead of slicked back. They were both tall, dark, and handsome men with a mysterious air about them. I'm sure my aunt loved that they were foreigners.

"She said you were both charmers. I can see that she was right." I narrowed my eyes slightly. They were both too smooth for my liking. "Well, gentlemen, I have to be going. Oh, and I wouldn't get anything off that rack. My aunt hates that kind of jewelry. She prefers black. I would go with Onyx."

"Thank you, Mon Cherie." Antoine winked.

"Until we meet again, Mon Amour." Louis blew me a kiss.

I waved and left without another word, but a small smile tipped up the corners of my lips as I headed across the room.

My aunt hated black.

Wolfgang spotted me and started whining and wiggling until I reached him.

"Are you being a naughty boy?" I patted the top of his head and used that as my excuse for hand sanitizer. Admittedly, that was part of the reason, but mostly I wanted to scrub the sleezy *charmers'* germs from my palms.

Milly rubbed her belly, which was getting bigger by the day. "He's not naughty. He's a good boy. He's just a little too much for me today."

"Well, thank you for calling me. I'll finish his walk and drop him at daycare." I tightened my jacket.

"Sounds good. I'll see you later. I'm going to take a nap then I'll head to daycare to relieve Dino. Watching dogs in a confined space is much easier than being pulled along on a walk. Besides, Dino has plans."

My forehead knitted. "Did he and Raven make up?"

Milly looked confused for a minute. "What do you mean?"

I studied her curiously. "She looked upset yesterday when you ran into her at Full Disclosure."

Milly's eyes widened a moment, then she cleared her throat, her cheeks flushing slightly pink. "Oh, right. Yes, they're better. He said he had a late lunch date later, so that's probably who he's meeting."

"Gotcha." I touched my chin with my finger for a moment, thinking, then said, "I'm curious. Who was the woman you rode off with yesterday? Is she new to town? I don't think I've ever met her."

"Just a fellow dog lover." Milly looked at her watch. "Oh, look at the time. I'd better lie down if I'm going to get a nap in." She handed the leash to me, and our hands touched. *Pulling this off is going to be harder than I thought.* She dropped her hand.

Pulling what off? I eyed her suspiciously before responding, "Of course. Thanks again, Milly. I'll see you later." I guided Wolfgang outside. Clearly something was going on with Milly that she didn't want to talk about. I certainly wasn't one to judge, as I was harboring a secret of my own.

Outside on Main Street, Wolf and I headed down the street in the direction of Dino's Daycare to finish his walk. At first, he started out just fine. Then the next thing I knew, he dropped his nose to the ground.

Sniffing like crazy, he picked up speed, pulling me along after him.

"Wolf, what on earth has gotten into you?" I huffed as I jogged along after him, trying to avoid people on the sidewalk. I uttered apologies and received a few strange looks, but Wolf trudged on with a determined gait.

More kibble.

He gobbled up piece after piece. Who would leave a trail of kibble and why? We got close to the end of the street, and the bushes started rustling. Oh, my Zeus, what if a rodent was in there? I dug my heels in and tried to stop, but Wolf lunged forward.

At the last second, two bodies dressed all in black popped out of the bushes.

A large net flung over Wolfgang and me.

I screamed.

Wolf growled.

The Ninja culprits yelled like banshees.

"Aha, we got you! You no make purse out of puppies on *my* watch," said one figure, giving the net a good tug.

"Wow, Cru-smella got a big one!" said the other figure, waving a hand in the air and taking a big step back.

Unbelievable. "Ma? Aunt Tasoula?" I gasped. "Get me out of this net right this minute." Pop was right. They really were crazy.

"Kalliope?" Ma dropped the net and rushed forward, pulling the black scarf off her lopsided beehive. "Is that you?"

"Kalli, why you napping with puppies?" Aunt Tasoula tsked as she pulled the net off me. "Oh, *that* no puppy. That smelly boy Wolf of the gangs." She wrinkled her nose, the black grease surrounding her eyes making her look like a racoon.

I glared at them both. "I'm *not* Cru-smella, and you two have some explaining to do."

AUNT TASOULA and Ma walked with me the rest of the way to Dino's Daycare to drop Wolfgang off first before we headed to Hera's Halo. The crime scene investigators had finished investigating the scene. While my aunt was still on strict orders not to leave town, she had the go ahead to reopen her business.

She had bills to pay, after all, and was the only hair salon in town. Not to mention, she employed her spa people, Rosy the nail technician and Perry the masseuse. They'd been operating out of their own homes with Aunt Tasoula's permission, but everyone was ready to get back to work.

"What are Vicky and Jasper doing here?" I asked, noticing her truck and his car parked out front.

"Oh, woe is me," Aunt Tasoula cried. "Hera needs a new halo. She traumatized over that murder. She lost her sparkle."

"It's true," Ma said gravely. "Skylar the flyer flew like tornado, doing all kinds of damage." She made the sign of the cross.

"I no wish Skylar dead, but the karmama got her. It always does." Aunt Tasoula bowed her head, her hands folded in prayer as she took a moment of silence that lasted all of two seconds before she shot me an excited smile. "Vicky and Jasper good eggs. They fix Hera right up for me."

"They *are* good eggs. They should get married and make Greek babies," Ma said with stars in her eyes.

"How?" I asked. "Neither one of them are Greek."

The stars left Ma's eyes as they hardened and sharpened on me. "Jasper Ballas *my* Greek baby just like you, Kalliope Ballas." She snapped her spine straight and patted her bosom. "That Greek enough for me."

"Okay, then." I was wise enough to know when to remain silent as I followed my ma and aunt inside the hair salon.

Aunt Tasoula squealed and clapped her hands as she spun around in a circle, taking everything in. Jasper and Vicky had fixed the damage and added a new coat of paint. "Hera's Halo look all shiny and new."

"Don't touch this wall. It's still wet." Jasper dropped the paint roller into a tray and carried it over to the sink.

"I'm so glad you like it." Vicky smiled wide as she walked out of the back room, sliding her hammer back into her tool belt and adjusting her strawberry blond ponytail. "I fixed Hera's throne in the back as well."

"Oh, good. And I love it." My aunt's eyes were wide with wonder.

"Did something happen, Ma?" Jasper asked, looking concerned as he joined us after cleaning up the paint.

Ma's eyes melted over his use of *Ma*, then she drew her eyebrows together when his words sank in. "What you mean, little one?"

I tried not to roll my eyes as I stood next to my fully-grown-far-from-little brother. Raising an eyebrow high, I sighed.

He shot me a look, then shrugged with a wink. "You and Aunt Tasoula are both dressed in black as if you are in mourning. I thought maybe something was wrong."

"Oh, something is very wrong," I said, earning his curious gaze and a scowl from Ma and Aunt Tasoula.

"Ah, you a good son to be concerned about you mama." Ma ignored me and smoothed her hands down her black polyester pantsuit, then her hand fluttered over her heart. "We *are* in mourning for the babies."

"Oh, yes. It's true. We set trap to catch nappers, but you sister in a gang with a wolf. She ruin everything, now babies doomed forever." Aunt Tasoula's shoulders slumped. "Those poor mamas gonna be milled by Cru-smella and have 202 more babies."

Jasper scratched his head, his lips parting as he looked at me.

"Don't ask." I rubbed my temples.

"Well, as long as you're good with everything, we need to get going." Vicky looked at her watch then turned to Jasper. "I have a couple more side jobs, then I'll meet you back at Aphrodite's."

"For a date?" Ma wagged her eyebrows at them.

Vicky blinked.

I scowled.

Jasper cleared his throat. "Actually, Pop wants us to renovate the patio."

Ma smiled wider. "He a good man."

"He's something," I said, wondering what Pop was up to.

"He sure is." Aunt Tasoula glared out the window.

"Amos not here." Ma shuffled over to my aunt and joined her at the window. "Who you look at?" She peered outside and sucked in a sharp breath. "Oh, no."

Aunt Tasoula stabbed her finger against the glass, her face three shades of red. If I didn't know better, I would swear her teased hair grew three inches in height. We all joined her to see what was happening.

Tate Hemsworth was strolling down the street, arm-in-arm with Hannah Schwarts, heads bent close together, deep in conversation. Suddenly, he stopped right in front of Hera's Halo and faced Hannah, taking her hands in his own.

"He wouldn't dare," Aunt Tasoula ground out.

What on earth was he up to? I wondered.

A gust of wind swept down the street, stirring up blades of grass and flower petals like something out of the movies...or a reality TV show. With a sideward glance at Hera's Halo storefront window, Tate locked eyes with my aunt and then smiled wide, having the gall to give her a wink. Then he focused back on Hannah, and he ceremoniously handed her a rose...and she accepted.

Let the games begin.

11

———

I was the first to arrive at Flannigan's Pub for our monthly girls' night out. Flannigan's was a cool Irish pub with rich wood, low lighting, gorgeous pictures of Ireland on the walls, and an Irish band playing in the corner of the dance floor. Old-fashioned Irish pub food sent aromas throughout the bar, making my stomach growl.

Flannigan's was my favorite spot to hang out. The elders of our Greek families rarely frequented the place, but all our cousins did. It was nice knowing there was a place to escape the mamas, especially during spring fever.

I pulled out a sanitized wipe and discreetly wiped off a stool before sitting at the bar where Silas's girl-friend Zena tended bar. She spotted me then poured a glass of chardonnay and carried it over.

"Right on time as usual." She smiled wide, her mischievous eyes sparkling.

People thought she was a pushover with her petite size and short blond pixie hairdo, but she could hold her own with her bold personality. She was the only woman who had ever been able to keep my charming cousin in line.

"Being late would give me anxiety." I shuddered in mock exaggeration and took a sip of my chardonnay.

She laughed. "I'm the same way." Then she arched a blond brow high. "I guess your cousin didn't inherit that trait."

"Why, is he supposed to be here?" I looked around but didn't see Silas or any of my other first cousins.

She glanced at her watch. "He was going to stop by first before he and Kosmos went down the street to Clearview Cigar Bar. They don't want to intrude on girls' night, but Silas wanted to see me since we've been so busy lately."

"Smart man." I winked.

Right on cue, Silas led the way in front of Kosmos and Winnie, with a guilty look on his face. "Sorry, doll face. Kos made me go through inventory with him before he would let us call it a night." He walked behind the bar as if he owned the place, wrapped Zena in his arms, then gave her a bear hug and big kiss.

"Quit harassing my best lass, Ballas," Michael Flannigan said as he walked out of his office and stepped behind the bar. The note of humor in his tone lessened the severity of his mock scowl.

Silas held his hands in the air and widened his eyes dramatically. "I don't know what you're talking about, Flannigan."

Zena laughed and shooed him out from behind the bar. "You can make it up to me later, Casanova."

"If someone had done his job earlier like I asked him, we wouldn't be late," Kosmos interjected, steering the conversation back to us.

"We're here now, mate, and that's all that matters." Winnie, the tall, voluptuous redhead, leaned over and kissed Kosmos then slid onto the stool beside me.

"Have fun, ladies." Kosmos waved, and then the

men left to join Nik and Boomer for cigars and poker down the street.

"What'd I miss?" Winnie asked.

"Nothing much. Just waiting on Jaz, Leni, and Thalia. Claudett can't make it. She and Yanni are out of town at a landscaping convention." I smiled fondly as my heart filled with joy. "I'm so happy for Yanni. Claudett seems perfect for him. He deserves to be happy after all he's been through." He was my oldest cousin. His first wife had died years ago, and he hadn't been the same since. Until he met Claudett. She used to be a party planner, but then they fell in love, and she went to work with him.

"That's wonderful," Winnie said. "He seems like such a great bloke. He deserves to have a good sheila of his own."

"He's always been on the serious side, but he's a great guy. He would do anything for anyone."

A man stepped behind the bar, tying an apron around his waist, drawing our attention.

"Finally," Zena said as her replacement relieved her. She untied her apron and joined us by the bar. "Follow me, ladies, I have a table set up for us over there." She pointed to the far wall where we had a view of the entire pub.

We no sooner sat down than Jaz and Thalia walked through the front door. Zena waved, and the women spotted us. Weaving their way through the crowd of people, they ordered a drink at the bar and sat down at our table.

"Sorry we're late," Jaz said. "I was going over paperwork with Thalia for the new house."

Thalia tucked her thick, bobbed hair behind her ears. "Buying a house never gets old. Very exciting times."

"It is definitely exciting." Jaz beamed. "We can't wait to move in."

"Speaking of moving in," Zena bit her lower lip before blurting, "Silas asked me to move into his apartment with him."

I sucked in a little breath. "Oh, wow, are you going to?"

"I'm thinking about it." Zena shrugged. "Everything is going so great between us, I'm afraid to mess anything up. I don't want him to get bored with me."

"Not a chance. I've seen the way that bloke looks at you. He's smitten." Winnie sighed dreamily. "I would jump at the chance to live with Kosmos. He just takes things at a slower pace. And, well, we've only been official for almost six months." Her brow furrowed. "I just hope he remembers our anniversary."

"I'm sure he will, honey." Thalia squeezed her hand. "You're a queen."

"Awe thank you."

"Speaking of romance," Jaz said. "How's the senator?"

Thalia laughed. "Parker is a character, that's for sure." She shrugged. "We'll see how things go."

I looked around at the full bar. "Where is Leni? She's never usually this late. I talked to her earlier, and she said she definitely had tonight off."

"Maybe she's with the medical examiner." Thalia rubbed her hands together. "He sure is a cutie."

"You sound like Ma." I shook my head.

The front door to the bar opened, and Leni walked in with a man.

"Hey, that's not Clint Davis." Jaz frowned.

"Nope, that sure isn't." I studied the familiar man with blond hair, dimples, and intelligent green eyes.

"I don't think he's local, but I have seen him around town," Zena said. "He's usually alone."

"Gary told me he's in town for the festival." I searched my memory until it came to me. "His name is Nolan Ryder."

I watched them stop in the middle of the dance floor as Tate and Hannah twirled past them. Good thing Aunt Tasoula wasn't there. Nolan and Leni had their heads bent close together in conversation over the loud music. For a moment, I thought they might dance, but then Leni smiled and said something to him. Nolan tilted his head in a bow, flashing those deep dimples, then he headed to the bar.

She looked around for a moment, then walked our way after spotting us. As soon as she reached our table, we all sat staring at her, waiting.

"What?" Her cheeks pinkened.

"Oh, no you don't. You're not getting off that easy." Thalia pointed at her. "First, you're single, and now you have not one but two hotties vying for your attention. You're blushing, and we want details."

"There's nothing to tell, and that's the frustrating part." Leni took a big sip of her margarita. "Clint comes into Aphrodite's all the time, and always sits in my section. He flirts, at least that's what I think he's doing, but then he never asks me on a date." She looked over at Nolan, sitting at the bar, and their eyes locked.

He waved.

She blushed deeper.

"How does Nolan Ryder come into the picture?" I asked.

Leni shrugged. "I've run into him a couple times around town, and today he came into Aphrodite's for dinner. When my shift ended, he asked me to go for a drink. I told him I was headed here for a girls' night, but that I would love a raincheck. We walked here together, and well, that's that."

The door opened once more, and this time, in walked a stunning vision with platinum blond hair. Grant Kingsley's wife, Blair, but he was nowhere in sight. For once, she wasn't hiding out at the hotel, but she was very much alone.

She looked around the pub as if on a mission, then her eyes locked onto Nolan's, and she made a beeline in his direction. He kept his gaze on hers, as he gestured to the stool next to him, and she took a seat.

Leni sighed. "So much for that raincheck."

THE NEXT DAY I was on my way to drop Wolfgang off at daycare. He loved his time playing with other dogs. He stopped to sniff the ground by some bushes, and I had a moment of PTSD. I tightened my hand on his leash when I heard rustling. The day was sunny and warm, eerily still like everything was frozen in time.

Then something jumped out of the bushes, and I screamed.

A squirrel ran past my feet and up a tree.

I took several calming breaths then looked Wolf in the eye. "Listen, buddy, you and I need to have a serious conversation." I pointed at him. "No more stopping by bushes. All this adrenaline can't be good for my insides, okay?"

He tilted his massive head to the side and whined.

"All right let's go play with your friends. No more detours." I led the way further down the street and could see the daycare. This time, I was the one who stopped short at the sight before me.

Hannah paced in front of Dino's Doggie Daycare with Dino hot on her heels. She turned around and they ran into each other. She held up her hands for him to stop. Then they started talking, calmly at first, then their hands started gesturing more wildly as they spoke. He shook his head no. She said something else, and he shook his head no again. Finally, Hannah threw her hands up in the air and marched away, her strides brisk and heavy with clear frustration. I didn't even know Hannah and Dino knew each other.

What on earth was that about?

I started to walk again, but then Raven pulled up to the curb right after as if she'd witnessed the whole thing and was waiting for Hannah to leave. Dino climbed into her car. I watched her point at Hannah walking down the street, and Raven's body language definitely gave off angry vibes. Dino scrubbed his head and shrugged. They started arguing. I couldn't hear what they were saying because the windows were closed, then they drove away.

What on earth was going on?

I continued the rest of the way into the daycare where Milly was hard at work. She was looking more and more tired and stressed lately. That couldn't be good in her condition. I imagined her husband made more than enough money to support them with his jewelry store profits, so I didn't really understand why she was putting herself through the stress of continuing to work at the daycare.

"Hey, Milly, Wolf's ready for his playdate." I handed her his leash. "Every day I can tell something is wrong. He misses Chanel and Versace, but I'm sure he'll have fun with whoever's back there."

"His Samoyed buddies, Cozmo and Caya, are waiting for him out back in the play yard. The black labs he loves, Max and Marley, are there as well. And his little dachshund girlfriends, Luna and Sunny, will be thrilled. They all get along so well, no matter their size or breed. Sometimes I think dogs are the better species. Human beings can be pure evil." She sighed, looking a little frazzled.

"Dogs are so smart. They know when something's wrong."

"They sure are smart. People forget they have real feelings and are sensitive to their owners' moods. Some people don't deserve to have pets." She handed Wolf off to one of the employees then arched her back and rubbed her muscles.

Wow, Milly was usually so positive. Maybe it was the pregnancy hormones. "Are you okay? Maybe you should sit down."

She sat down at the chair behind the front desk and rubbed her temples. "I'm just tired." She looked past me.

I followed her gaze but didn't see anyone. "Are you expecting anyone?"

"No, just waiting for Dino to come back in so I can go home. I opened to take care of the boarding dogs. It's been a long morning."

I frowned. "Does he know he's supposed to relieve you because he just left with Raven in her car."

Milly blinked. "Excuse me?"

"You mean you didn't know he was going somewhere?" What boss would just assume his employee was okay with staying later. He didn't seem like the type to take advantage of people, then again, they had history together. Maybe he figured she wouldn't mind covering for him in a pinch.

"He never said a word," she muttered. "That's not like him."

"Do you think something's wrong?"

She hesitated a moment as if she wanted to say something, but then just said, "I'm sure everything is okay. Something must have come up."

"I saw Hannah talking with him out front. Their conversation looked intense before she stormed off. Then Raven pulled up, picked up Dino, and I didn't have to hear them talking to know they argued before they drove off."

"Hannah doesn't have any pets. I'm surprised she was here." Milly shrugged. "Maybe she was just here to see Dino."

"If I didn't know better, I would think they were in a love triangle," I speculated, "but Hannah is a lot older than Dino."

"Age is just a number," Milly said. "We've seen proof of that. Look at Grant. He's old enough to be his wife's father."

"True, but I also saw Hannah and Tate dancing at Flannigan's Pub last night. And he gave her a rose the other day in front of my aunt's shop. Either he's playing games trying to make my aunt jealous, or he and Hannah are really dating. If that's the case, then what do Hannah and Dino have in common?"

"I don't know what to think anymore." Milly paused then cleared her throat. "I'm sure everything is fine." Her phone dinged with a text message. She frowned. "I have to make a call, but I'll have Wolf ready by the end of the day." She headed into the office and shut the door.

Everything is fine?

Something told me everything wasn't fine. If I were a betting woman, I would wager something was very, very wrong.

"So, where do you want to go for lunch today?" Jaz asked me as we walked down Main Street, hanging more flyers with Chanel, Versace, and the puppies' pictures and information. Someone must have seen something, but so far, no one was talking. After finding the perfect house, Jaz's determination to find her dogs had grown even more.

"Hmmm, good question, and perfect timing." My stomach growled, and I groaned. "See. I'm starving."

"Me, too. Walking and hanging flyers is exhausting. I think we covered every street in this town."

"My feet sure feel like we have, but I'm not complaining. I will do anything to help you find your precious girls and all our babies. I would be a wreck if Prissy or, yes, even Wolfgang went missing." I stapled a flyer to a telephone pole and kept walking. "I was thinking we should go someplace we haven't been in a while."

I spotted a building down the road. "What about Vincenzo's? We never get to go there because of Ma's and Vinny's feud. But now that they're on a truce, this would be a great opportunity." I loved Italian food but saying that to Ma would be sacrilegious. So, when Nik and I want Italian, we cooked it ourselves.

"Let's go, then. It's right here. I'm game if you are, since we might not get another chance." Jaz grinned and grabbed my hand, pulling me after her. *I'm so hungry, this is going to taste amazing.*

I laughed and let her lead the way.

We entered Vincenzo's, and it felt like stepping back in time to ancient Italy. The aroma of basil, oregano, and garlic permeated the air, making my mouth water. We headed over to the hostess station and requested a table for two. We were about to be seated when a loud commotion sounded in the kitchen.

Suddenly, Ma came storming out of the kitchen, her face flushed and beehive lopsided, with Drake and Vinny hot on her heels.

"You can't just barge into my restaurant and enter my kitchen, Ophelia Ballas." Vincenzo Ricci talked with his hands every step of the way. He wasn't much taller than Ma, with a big belly and thick, black hair slicked back that matched his mustache. He'd graduated in Ma's class in high school.

"Drake suppose to be with *me* today, but I see his car here. You steal Drake away. He Tasoula's friend, no yours." She pointed her finger in his face. "He supposed to show *me* his cooking cracks, no you."

"First of all, it's cooking hacks, not cracks. Second, I didn't steal anyone away. He came to me." Vinny patted his chest.

Ma turned to Drake who paled under her glare. "Is this true, Drake Fontanna? Are you traitor?"

"What can I say? I'm Italian, not Greek." Drake held up his hands. "I would be a traitor if I betrayed my own country."

"You definitely no Greek." Ma thrust her chin in the air, looking down her nose at him in disgust. "And you a traitor to you friends."

"Who says Vinny isn't my friend?" Drake stood his ground against Ma. "Besides, Vinny's letting me use his kitchen after hours."

"All you have to do is ask, but you turn traitor. You in bed with the enemy," Ma spat. "Now, you no use my anything."

"I'm not in bed with anyone." Drake threw his hands up and let out a big puff of air. He stood there with his hands on his hips, pausing as if counting to ten before finally responding, "It's nothing personal, Ophelia."

"Cooking is *always* personal." Ma poked him in the chest.

Drake frowned. "Wanna know the real reason I didn't want to use your kitchen?" He pointed at her but drew short of poking her back.

Smart man.

Ma narrowed her eyes. "Why?"

"Because of her." He thrust his finger in my direction.

Oh, boy.

Ma's surprised gaze shot to me and Jaz as if just now realizing we were there and what that meant. She just stood still with wide eyes that moved from me to Jaz and back to me again, her mouth gaping open with her canine teeth looking larger and sharper than normal.

Jaz and I stood frozen, looking guilty as sin.

Jaz grabbed my arm, showing all her teeth to Ma in a massive smile. *Say something now before Morticia eats us.*

I snapped out of my stupor and waved, pasting a big smile on my face. "Hi Ma, fancy seeing you here."

Ma snapped her jaw closed harder than a shark as she crossed her arms and narrowed her eyes to slits. "Kalliope Ballas and Jazlyn Alvarez, what in Mount Olympus you two doing eating with the enemy?"

"We're not," Jaz blurted, her face turning pale. "We were looking for you, Mrs. Ballas. We would never eat here. The food is yucky." She shook her head no at Vinny and mouthed sorry after Ma looked at me.

"Is that true, Kalliope?" Ma stared me down.

My shoulders slumped and my feet were killing me. I was exhausted, and I was over all the drama. "Honestly, Ma, I can't keep up with you." I rubbed my temples, wondering what that much throbbing against my brain might do to me long term. "I thought you and Mr. Ricci were on a truce."

"No truce!" both she and Vinny shouted at the same time.

"And now no food for you two, either." Vinny pointed at Jaz and me. "You're both just as crazy as this loon."

"Fine, whatever. I'm over it all. You two have the strangest relationship." I shook my head and turned to Drake. "Why am I involved in this latest dispute?" I stared at Drake with raised hands.

"Your boyfriend keeps prying into my business, that's why." He took a step toward me as his hands slightly clenched, but I saw.

He had a temper. Was he capable of murder?

"Your face is an open book," he went on. "I can tell what you're thinking, but I can promise you I didn't have anything to do with Skylar's murder." He loosened his hands and stood a little straighter. "Who I spend my time with is none of you or your detective boyfriend's business."

"It is when it's Ursula Smith." I kept calm and let my words sink in, but unlike me, Drake had a great poker face. "Ursula is a suspect in Skylar's murder as well. I overheard you talking outside of Sal's Supermarket in the parking lot. If you have nothing to hide, tell me what you two are involved in."

"I don't know what you're talking about," he said a little too quickly. "I'm not doing anything with Ursula Smith. I don't even like the woman. And I know my rights. I'm not telling you anything."

"Is that what Ursula advised you to say?" She'd said pretty much the same thing to me, and she was a successful criminal defense attorney.

He stared me down. I didn't have to read his mind to know he was mentally pleading the fifth.

"It doesn't matter what you say, Mr. Fontana. I *will* find out what's going on between you two and prove my aunt is innocent."

"You're all crazy." Drake looked at me, Ma, Jaz, and Vinny then shrugged. "Nothing shady is going on. I simply needed an industrial kitchen to test out some of my recipes, that's all, but you two are *not* the only kitchens in town. And you're definitely not worth the effort." He stormed out without a single glance back.

"Rosalita no help you," Ma shouted after him. "She loyal."

Drake just shook his head but kept walking.

Ma grunted, let loose a string of Greek words, then turned to Vinny with a glare. "That no mean our truce over."

"Fine by me." Vinny's jaw clenched. "I don't have to steal anyone for my restaurant to be the best." He looked down his nose at her.

"Let's go, girls." Ma stared at Jaz and me, daring us to disobey her.

We looked at each other and sighed. We were smarter than that. You didn't want to mess with an angry Greek mama when it came to food. We headed outside just in time to see Drake get into Ursula's car and drive off together.

So much for him not liking the woman.

~

"SHE HAVE SOME NERVE," Aunt Tasoula said that afternoon in Hera's Halo as she trimmed Jaz's hair.

The new renovations looked great, and my aunt seemed happy to have her salon back. If she was worried about going to jail, she sure hid it well. At times I saw a glimpse of vulnerability which made me wonder how she really felt, but pretending everything was fine was her defense mechanism.

My aunt didn't deal well with reality.

"Who has nerve?" I asked, playing along.

I'd tagged along with Jaz for a manicure. Jaz had bought me a mani-pedi for my birthday, and I still hadn't used it, so she insisted I did so today. I set my backpack down and sat at Rosy the nail tech's station which was just beyond the hair stylist chairs.

"Hannah Schmannah," my aunt ground out, snipping away at Jaz's hair. "She come in. Want me to style her hair after she take rose from *my* man. Right in front of *my* shop. That disrespect."

"Don't forget dancing at Flannigan's," Jaz pointed out before I could stop her. "Those two can really cut a rug."

"See, they fools." Aunt Tasoula clicked her scissors

in the air to make a point. "Why cut perfectly good rug?"

Jaz blinked.

I rolled my eyes.

Jaz shrugged. "Anyway, they danced for hours. I don't remember them leaving the dance floor the whole time during girls' night out. Do you, Kalli?" She looked at me innocently.

I wisely stayed silent.

She must have read my expression. "Or maybe it wasn't them. Yeah, it could have been someone else?"

I arched my brow at her, again silently.

She sheepishly gave me an apologetic wince. Tate looked like a giant blond Viking. There was no *mistaking* him. I hadn't told my aunt what had happened that night because I knew it would only make her even more upset.

Aunt Tasoula's eyes widened when Jaz's words finally sank in, then her face twisted into an angry expression. "There only one blond Hercules in town. That have to be him. That man make me so mad I could disintegrate."

"Detonate?" Jaz wrinkled her nose.

"Explode?" I asked.

"All of them." My aunt's face looked purple, and her ears whistled like her favorite centaur teapot.

"Have you told him how you feel?" I asked gently.

"I no chase man. If he want Skylar the flyer and Hannah the spinning top, then he no man for me."

"I thought you were seeing Clayton Brown?" I rolled my aching head on my shoulders, feeling tense. My family was making me crazy, and I still couldn't shake the feeling that someone was following me. Not to mention, how could Aunt Tasoula even think about dating anyone when she was a suspect in a murder investigation? She had a crazy way of coping with stress.

When life handed her lemons...she handed out batons.

My aunt pondered my question for a moment as her face finally returned to its normal rosy color, and I relaxed about her blood pressure. "I dating Clayton... sort of. I gave him the most batons, but I think he fake."

"Why?"

"I know a wig when I see one. He never get hair trimmed. It always look the same." She leaned forward and lowered her voice. "I think he bald."

"I think bald men are beautiful," Jaz said. "Have you seen how many bald movie stars there are who are the leading heartthrobs?"

"Me know, and I tell him, but he no let me help." Aunt Tasoula shrugged. "I no cut a rug. Someday I just rip it off." She snapped her fingers. "Or maybe I burn it with my baton like Principal Wimble."

"Oh, my Zeus, don't do that, Aunt Tasoula," I blurted, jerking a hand and smudging my manicure, earning a disapproving frown from Rosy. "Sorry," I said to Rosy, then gave my aunt a pointed look. "You're already in enough trouble. We don't need you arrested for anything else, okay?"

"Trouble Shmubble." My aunt blew me off and continued to style Jaz's hair, but I could tell by the tenseness in her shoulders my words had hit home.

She was more worried than she let on.

"What about those handsome French brothers," Jaz asked, oblivious to what was really going on with my aunt. "They seem to be into you. I bet they would accept your batons." She winked.

Aunt Tasoula wrinkled her nose. "They okay, but

they get me black jewelry. With all the beautiful colors in the rainbow, they get me black. I no wear black. They have some making up to do for more batons."

The bell over the front door chimed and in walked the devils themselves.

The Dupont brothers.

The men smiled wide, but I didn't trust them. Their teeth were too straight and white, their hair perfectly styled, their words practiced and polished. One carried a gorgeous bouquet of colorful flowers and the other a case of gourmet chocolates.

"For you, Mon Cherie." Antoine handed my aunt the bouquet.

Her eyes widened. "For me? They so beautiful."

Louis handed her the box of chocolates. "We got better advice on what you might like this time, je t'aime." His gaze shot to mine and hardened before softening as he turned back to my aunt. "What else can we do to make it up to you?"

My aunt's eyes twinkled with delight. "Surprise me." She let out a high-pitched trilling giggle that made me wince it was so ear-piercing.

The brothers looked at each other and a small smiled tipped up the corners of their lips as they said in unison, "Done."

First of all, I didn't like the smug satisfaction that passed between the men. And second, I had a sneaking suspicion I wasn't going to like what they had in mind. I was afraid my aunt was in over her head.

Maybe it was time I did something about it.

13

———

"**Y**ou too thin, Kalli." Ma pinched my ribs after I'd hardly eaten at the buffet table beneath the gazebo in her back yard. The sky was cloudy, but there wasn't any rain in the forecast. Lately, the feeling of being followed had intensified. I refused to let it dictate my actions.

It was Sunday brunch again, and the whole family was there. Leni had even brought Clint. Nolan had asked her on a date, but she'd gotten a bad taste in her mouth the night he was at Flannigan's Pub with Grant's wife Blair, so she'd turned him down and asked Clint out herself instead. She'd gotten sick of waiting around for him to ask her. Apparently, he was shy.

The only ones who weren't there were Jasper and Vicky. Jasper went to church but left to work on the patio addition to Aphrodite's, while Vicky was finishing up in the back room of Aunt Tasoula's salon.

"I had a snack before church," I lied, hoping Father Papadopoulos couldn't tell, but he was across the yard talking to my biological father, Father Connery.

Ma tsked, shaking her beehive. "Those recreations killing you."

After Jaz and Boomer had moved out, Nik and I had resumed our renovations to make our two apartments into one home. We still didn't talk about what our future would look like beyond moving in together, but we knew we were both ready to at least take this step.

"Those *renovations* are not what's killing me." My ma, my aunt, and Nik's ma would not stop sneaking into our house and making it more *Greek*. "First, you leave statues we don't want. You're trying to install a fountain in the yard. And now you leave several crosses and rosary beads. You all need to stop."

Ma gasped and made the sign of the cross. "You no like the gods?"

"Of course, I do. That is what Sunday mass and brunch are all about. I don't need my house to look like our Greek Orthodox Church."

She shrugged and sniffed sharply. "Fine. But I no see you confess to Father Papadopoulos lately. You full of sins."

"Let's just focus on clearing Aunt Tasoula's name first." I was sure I would have plenty of sins to confess by the time I was through *interfering*, as Nik would say. "I'm really worried about her."

"She okay." Ma looked over at my aunt twirling her baton in front of Clayton. "She just put on the showbiz."

I watched my aunt twirl the baton dangerously close to his hair, as if trying to knock something off his head, but he kept ducking out of the way just in time. "I'm not so sure. She doesn't seem herself."

"She boy crazy. She always boy crazy ever since we little. She be fine." Ma shrugged. "She think she *is* the fountain of youth. She afraid to get old."

"I think she's acting even crazier than usual because she's afraid she might go to prison." The baton slipped and finally made contact with Clayton's head, and my eyes widened when it looked like his hairline was slightly crooked now.

Maybe he really was bald and embarrassed to let her know.

He jumped to his feet, bowed to her slightly while being careful not to tilt his head too far forward, and kissed the back of her hand before taking his leave. Aunt Tasoula frowned as she watched him leave then she shrugged and headed our way, her tassels swinging with every sparkly step.

Ma's hand fluttered to her chest. "Oh, my Hades," she said on a woosh of air. "She no gonna make it behind the bars."

"Is something wrong with Mr. Brown?" I asked as my aunt dodged a singing Frona who bounced by on her pogo stick, shaking pom poms, and chanting a cheer.

Aunt Tasoula shook her baton and scowled at the disappearing pom poms before looking at me. "What you say?"

"How come Clayton left?" I clarified.

"He no feel well. He got the indiscretion." She rubbed her stomach.

"Ah, that no good." Ma shook her head gravely, her beehive swinging like a bobble head. "Cousin Neville have the indiscretion. He have black hole in stomach now. Never the same. Skinny. Food fall right out."

"Never the same," Aunt Tasoula repeated, making the sign of the cross.

"You okay, 'Soula?" Ma patted her sister's shoulder. "I hear if you need the talk. I good listener."

"He take the acid. He be okay."

"I think Ma means if you want to talk about your fears over how the murder investigation is going."

My aunt's eyes grew big for a moment, then she stiffened her spine. "I fine. I majorette. I professional." She thrust her baton in the air. "The show must go on."

Someone screamed when it fell on their head.

"There no show except the act you put on," Ma snapped, then she gentled her voice. "It okay to be afraid. I was afraid when I suspect, and so was Chloe."

"You were?" My aunt's shoulders drooped.

Ma nodded. "Prison scary place."

My aunt wailed, and her tears erupted, like an overflowing fountain. "I too pretty for jail."

Ma wrapped her in a hug. "There, there, 'Soula. You be okay. Kalli no let that happen." She walked away with my blubbering aunt, consoling her.

Kalli no let that happen...

No pressure. My stomach churned.

I knew Ma was right. My aunt would never survive prison, not to mention, I knew she was innocent. I'd *heard* the truth; besides, my aunt wasn't capable of murder no matter how many buttons of hers Skylar Delaney had pushed.

I clenched my jaw. Speaking of pushing buttons. Tate Hemsworth should be here right now, supporting my aunt, instead of gallivanting around with Hannah just to make my aunt jealous. He knew my aunt better than that. The only reason she'd said she wanted a break was because they were growing too close, and she hadn't loved anyone since Uncle Leon.

It was easier to push people away than to risk getting hurt.

My gaze found Nik through the crowd. I could relate. It was hard to fully break down my walls and let him in. He got me and loved me in spite of my flaws, but would he grow bored or annoyed with me over time? Every other man I'd ever cared about had let me down in the past, so I'd stopped caring...until him.

I was head-over-heels in love with Nikos Stevens.

Suddenly, he looked up and locked eyes with me. As if reading my mind, he mouthed, *I love you*, and my heart melted. I didn't want to fall into the same trap as my aunt. I didn't want to push Nik away in fear of getting hurt because spending my life without him would hurt far worse. I intended to tell him that as soon as this investigation was over with.

A breeze picked up, and it felt like the temperature was dropping. I zipped up my coat and tapped my watch then pointed to the road. He nodded once and started saying his goodbyes. Thirty minutes later, we met out front.

"Why is it always so impossible to leave brunch in less than a half hour?" Nik unlocked his car, and we slid inside.

"Because our big fat Greek families are huge," I said.

"And talkers," he pointed out.

"And huggers," I added.

"Can you imagine our wedding? Our honeymoon would be half over before they would let us go." He laughed.

I blinked.

Neither one of us spoke until we got home.

We climbed out of the car, and I shivered. There was a definite chill in the air now. Glancing at the sky, I noticed the clouds had turned a darker shade a gray. I pulled out my keys and hurried to unlock the door and step inside.

Silence.

Nik came in and nearly bumped into my back. "What's wrong?"

"Do you hear that?" I looked up at him.

He arched a brow. "Hear what?"

"Exactly." I looked around.

He frowned then headed into the house before me. "Wolf?" He whistled. "Here, boy. Where are you? Want a treat?"

Still silence. Nik's gaze met mine with genuine concern.

"Prissy?" I called, my heart beginning to race.

Not a single hiss or meow.

We searched both halves of our house from top to bottom, but they were nowhere to be found. Good thing Jaz and Boomer weren't still living here. This would trigger them for sure. No words were necessary for Nik and me to be on the same page.

He headed to his bedroom, and I headed to mine to change. I pulled on yoga pants, a sweatshirt, and sneakers. Putting my hair into a ponytail, I grabbed my raincoat and backpack, which always had all my gadgets, a flashlight, and a whistle.

Nik met me by the front door, dressed in joggers, sweatshirt, sneakers, and his gun. "Where to, Ballas?"

I pulled out my cell phone and hit the *Find My* app. My biggest fear was losing my pets, so when we'd decided to move in together, I had bought Wolf a tracking tag like Prissy's and put it in a holder on his collar. Pairing his with my cell phone like I had hers, I was able to click on the devices and see where our pets were at all times. As long as the tag was within anyone's Bluetooth range, I would be able to track them on my phone. But if they ventured out of range, deeper into the wilderness, we could lose them forever.

I blew out a breath of relief. "They're in the woods. We need to move while we're still in range."

Nik set his jaw. "Let's roll."

I followed him out the door. Our house butted up to the woods, so maybe the animals got out and headed that way, yet nothing was left open. All the mamas were at brunch, and there were no new surprises left in the house, so it couldn't have been them.

Someone must have pet-napped them.

Wolfgang and Prissy were purebreds, but they weren't puppies. What value could they hold? Or was someone trying to send a message? So many thoughts went through my mind, but beyond my fear was a fierce resolve. One thing these pet-nappers hadn't realized...

They'd messed with the wrong fur-parents.

~

AN HOUR LATER, Nik and I pulled off the side of the road on the outskirts of town. We had been driving along the edge of the woods, tracking the tags on my phone. Once the tags headed deeper into the woods, we knew we needed to venture in on foot.

The first fat raindrops fell from the sky.

I slipped my raincoat on and pulled up the hood, then slid my backpack on up over my shoulders. Holding my phone, I led the way. "It looks like they're trekking deeper into the woods."

"Their tracking tags are hidden in a waterproof holder on their collars." Nik had his gun in a holster at his waist, easy to reach if needed. "You'd have to know what you're looking for to realize what they are. Maybe we'll get lucky and catch the puppy-nappers in the act."

"Wolfgang is pretty strong and very protective. What if they got away and are all alone out there in the wild?" I kept walking over boulders, across streams, through unmarked trails of pinecone and needle covered ground. The trees had bloomed with lots of leaves by now. "I'm terrified that hungry bears with cubs fresh out of hibernation or packs of wolves looking for food will find them before we do."

"Like you said, Wolf is very protective and menacing when he wants to be. He won't let anything happen to Prissy." Nik's voice was firm and reassuring. "Stay strong, Ballas. We'll find them." His voice grew deep and gritty with a note of promise when he added, "But whoever took them won't want to find me."

Thunder rumbled and a streak of lightening lit up the sky as the rain picked up, and I shivered against the chill. Prissy would be so cold and scared and not happy about being wet. Suddenly, the tags stopped moving. "Why did they stop?" I jerked to a halt myself and looked at Nik.

"I don't know, but this is our chance to reach them." He looked at my phone's location, then took off at a jog.

I hurried to keep up.

We kept moving at a quick pace when we heard a low growl. Nik skidded to a stop and drew his weapon, motioning for me to be quiet. I froze, terrified of what that noise could come from. I saw a flash of gold seconds before a golden retriever appeared on the path in front of us. Nik blew out a breath of air and lowered his gun.

"Come here, boy," he called.

I pulled out the treat bag from my coat and shook it.

The dog didn't come. He just looked at us, then barked once more, and finally turned around to run off.

We quickly followed.

It didn't take long before we came upon a hunting cabin. I stopped and checked my phone. "Nik, the tags stop here."

"Stay behind me." Nik still had his gun lowered at an angle as we made our way slowly forward.

The door suddenly whipped open, and Malik Cooper stood there in all his glory, looking like The Black Panther, dressed in an onyx warmup suit with a matching knit hat on. "Midas, come," he said loudly with obvious frustration in his voice. He snapped his fingers and pointed to the ground in front of him.

The golden retriever trotted over immediately with its head hanging low.

"Bad boy," Keisha joined Malik in the doorway. "You don't run off like that. You're too valuable to us, do you hear me?" She pointed her finger at the dog's face.

The dog sat and whined.

"Well, get on in here, then." Malik ushered the dog inside and was about to close the cabin door.

Nik took a step forward with his gun still in his hand, and they both looked up in startled surprise.

"Detective Stevens?" Malik's lips parted.

"Ms. Ballas?" Keisha blinked.

"Is my dog in there, Cooper?" Nik ground out.

"And my cat?" I asked. "Do you have my cat?"

Malik looked at Keisha and then back at us as he responded, "Yes, but this isn't what it looks like."

"Well, this is." Nik stepped forward. "Malik and Keisha Cooper, you have the right to remain silent. Anything you say can and will be used against you in a court of law. You have the right to an attorney. If you cannot afford one, one will be provided for you. Do you understand these rights I have just read to you?"

"I understand you're arresting us," Malik said.

"What for?" Keisha added.

"Pet-napping," I said, pushing past them into the cabin to see four golden retrievers, one Saint Bernard, and one very wet and angry calico cat, but not a single poodle or Saint Berdoodle.

14

———

"Oh my gosh, I can't believe that just happened." Jaz sat on the floor of my living room, leaning against my couch, with Wolfgang's head in her lap.

As soon as Boomer heard the call come over the radio about Nik arresting Malik and Keisha Cooper for pet-napping, he'd met Nik at the station and Jaz had come straight over to help me. She'd bathed Wolfgang while I changed out of my own wet clothes and tended to Prissy. For once my calico cat had allowed me to cuddle her as she lay curled up in an exhausted orange, black, and white ball in my lap as I sat on my overstuffed chair. She hated baths, and this one had taken everything out of her.

"And I can't believe Nik had to let the Coopers go." I sighed. "They claim they were walking through the woods with their golden retrievers, working on training exercises, when the storm hit. They took shelter in a cabin they found, when one of their dogs escaped and Wolfgang and Prissy showed up."

"Do you really believe the Coopers rescued your pets rather than stealing them?" Jaz stroked Wolfgang's white, brown, and black fur over and over. He looked exhausted as his big, droopy eyes closed tight. He let out the occasional whine, but otherwise, he didn't move a muscle.

"I don't know what to believe." That was the truth. My brain was still processing everything that had happened. "Someone was in our house. Maybe they were looking for something and our pets escaped."

Jaz glanced around the room with wide wary eyes. "What could they have been looking for?"

"I don't have a clue. Maybe it was Skylar Delaney's real killer, and they think my aunt knows something. My aunt stops over occasionally and brings me products from her salon, but my ma and cousins are the same way. It's a Greek thing. They're always trying to feed and water me. Maybe they think she left something here. I don't know. I feel like I'm grasping at straws to make sense of all this."

"I don't blame you. I would be too. It gives me the creeps knowing someone was in your place." She shivered. "Same way with Boomer's apartment. I'll never think of that place as ours, and after the puppy-napping, I just want out. I can't wait until we get to move into our new house."

"I agree. I think for this house to feel like both Mine and Nik's place together, the remodel is essential. Even more so now after the break-in." I stroked Prissy's fur and she purred, leaning into my palm as I considered all options. "Here's another thought. Maybe the person doesn't have anything to do with the murder investigation. Maybe they really were just out to kidnap our pets."

"Then why let them go in the woods? I don't get it. There's no monetary value in doing that."

My gaze met hers as I voiced one of my biggest

fears. "Maybe to send a message for me to stop investigating?"

"You think so?" Her brow puckered and lips parted. "What would make you think something like that?"

"Well, I've had a strong feeling of being watched lately. I carry my backpack everywhere I go. I have so much stuff in there, I don't always go through it fully, so I'm not sure when this happened. I didn't tell this to Nik because then he would probably never let me leave the house again, but I found this in my backpack when I got home and changed." I pulled a note out of my sweatshirt pocket and showed Jaz.

Back off or else...

She gasped and gaped at the note. "That was in your backpack? Oh my gosh, how terrifying. What do you think that means?"

"I'm not sure what it means, and yes, it is terrifying." I studied the note once more, then tucked it away again. "It could mean the murder investigation or the puppy-napping or just about anything."

"When do you think someone slipped it into your backpack?" She looked around warily while petting Wolfgang.

I couldn't blame her. The thought of a threatening note was intimidating. "It could have been at work the time I found it unzipped. Or maybe church, or brunch, or the restaurant, or even the cabin in the woods. I hadn't emptied it fully until it got wet. I wanted to dry everything off. That's when I found the note, but who knows how long it has been in there."

"Are you afraid?" She bit her bottom lip.

I thought about that then took a deep breath. "I

was at first, but not so much now. I'm angry and more determined than ever."

"I get angry. I'm so relieved you got your pets back. I'm trying to stay determined, but it's difficult. I'm just sad with every day that goes by that mine are still missing. It's hard not to give up hope."

"Stay strong. Hope is all we have, so don't let that go." My cell phone rang, and we both jumped.

An annoyed Prissy stretched then leaped off my lap. Wolfgang let out a howl and then walked out of the room behind her. Jaz climbed up onto the couch and waited for me to answer my phone.

"Nik? You're on speaker. Jaz is here."

"Good. This message is for both of you. The rangers found something in one of the cabins in the woods."

"Is it the puppies?" Jaz asked.

"No, but there is animal fur at the scene. Someone has been squatting in an old sugar shanty all winter. We have a team dusting for prints and collecting evidence. If we find this person, maybe we'll find our puppy-napper."

"Thanks for letting us know," I said. "Keep us posted."

"Will do." He hung up.

"Pieces of fur?" Jaz swallowed hard. "What does that mean?"

"Don't let your mind jump to conclusions. We won't know anything until the evidence is analyzed."

"What are we supposed to do in the meantime?" Jaz wrung her hands together then jumped off the couch and began to pace.

"We hang more flyers around town, ask more questions, broaden our search." I looked her in the eyes. "We don't give up."

She nodded once. "Then let's get going."

THE RAIN FINALLY LET UP. After calling Vicky and having her change the locks on our house, I made sure our pets were secure then Jaz and I headed out. Nik and Boomer were checking out the sugar shanty while Jaz and I broadened our search for the puppies, hitting the businesses on the outskirts of town.

Lakeshore Heights was just across the town line. A small, quaint motel with cozy cabins down at the Oasis on a lake tucked into the woods. After realizing the puppies might have gone into the woods, we'd decided this motel would be a good place to look. It was worth a shot to at least see if there were any signs.

We parked in the parking lot at the motel and went inside. The interior was rustic with animal heads mounted on the wall. A man who looked to be in his sixties with chubby cheeks and a round belly gave us a big smile when we approached the front desk. His name tag said Arnold.

"Hi, Arnold, I'm Kalli Ballas." I reached out my hand and shook his.

"Nice to meet you." *Why do you look so familiar?*

"I met you not too long ago with my boyfriend, Detective Stevens, when we were here looking for his cousin Viggo."

Arnold's eyes widened and his smile vanished. He let go of my hand. "I don't want no trouble."

"We're not here to cause any trouble, sir." Jaz drew his wary gaze away from me as I sanitized my hands. She handed him a flyer. "We're here looking for puppies. Twenty-two Saint Berdoodles to be exact, and two full-sized black poodles."

He took the flyer from her and squinted to study the page closer, then started shaking his head. "I heard about this, but I ain't seen nothin' like these pups around here. Sorry." He held the sheet back out to her.

"Do you mind hanging that in your lobby? You never know who might stop in. Someone has to have seen something with that many dogs involved."

"Sure thing, Miss...?"

"Jaz Alvarez. Detective Matheson is my fiancé."

Arnold grunted. "Everybody's datin' the law these days." He stepped around his desk and hung the flyer on the bulletin board of events on the wall.

"Do you mind if we take a look down by the cabins?" I glanced round, but no one was in the lobby.

"Whatever floats your boat, lady. It's a free country. All I ask is that you don't bother my guests. People pay for privacy when they stay here."

Privacy. That was one way of putting it. "No worries. We will be very discreet." I handed him my card. "Please let me know if you hear anything at all about these puppies."

"You got it." He put my card in the drawer by the register.

Jaz and I headed outside.

"Where are we going," she asked.

"Down by the water." I led the way.

"What are we doing down there?" she whispered.

"Why are you whispering?" I laughed.

"I don't know." She laughed back. "Wouldn't want to *disturb* anyone in the cabins." She made a grimace.

"It's barely past supper. I doubt we'll be disturbing anyone this early. The sun is starting to go down so I wanted to see if we could find any paw prints down by the water before dark. There are woods all around here."

"Your pets have tracking tags, which I'm going to buy the second I get mine back, but you don't know the first thing about tracking without technology." Jaz studied the ground with every step. "What are we even looking for?"

"True, but twenty-two sets of tiny paw prints would be hard to miss if anyone had them here. Let's just see if we get lucky."

We kept walking until we finally got to the lake, then spent thirty minutes searching the area. Suddenly, we heard voices coming down the hill. I looked at Jaz, and some instinct had us both ducking behind the bushes of a cabin.

A man and woman were talking in whispers, so we couldn't hear what they said until they drew closer.

"No one will judge you. You have every right to be happy. You can't feel guilty about this," the man said.

"I know, you're right. I deserve better. I've been so patient, and given up so much, it's time I put myself first," the woman responded.

I looked at Jaz, and we both peeked through the branches, gaping in surprise. What were those two doing together? Nolan Ryder stood with his head close to Blair Kingsley. Other than expressing interest in my cousin Leni, I hadn't seen Nolan with anyone else besides Blair in Flannigan's Pub that one time.

Apparently, they'd hit it off.

This was so awkward. Jaz grabbed my hand. *Don't move. We look like peeping toms hiding in these bushes. Once they go inside, we can slip away.*

I nodded and stayed quiet.

Blair took a deep breath, and Nolan pulled out a... a camera. I looked at Jaz, and she shrugged. Blair put her hand on the door, and then seconds later, she flung it wide open. The flash on Nolan's camera went off like a strobe light.

A woman screamed.

A man cursed.

Blair yelled, "Gotcha," as she stepped inside the cabin with Nolan hot on her heels, clicking the camera every step of the way.

Jaz and I stood up and peeked through the cabin window. Grant Kingsley and Chelsea Turner were hiding beneath the sheets of the king size bed in the middle of the room.

"Blair, I can explain." Grant ran a hand through his messy hair.

"There is no good explanation for why you would cheat on me with this old woman." Blair pointed at Chelsea with her silver hair tucked behind her ears.

"I am hardly old, dear. Don't you know that natural hair is in?" Chelsea raised a brow. "I highly doubt that bottle blond you're sporting is natural. I guess you don't know better, since you're just a child."

"Chelsea, you're not helping." Grant looked at her in frustration.

"But you said you were going to leave her for me." Chelsea pouted.

"Please do," Blair ground out. "I've wasted twelve years on you, but no more. Now I'm entitled to half of what you're worth."

"Baby, you don't mean that." Grant yanked on his pants beneath the covers and then stood. "What about the children?"

"You should have thought of them before taking me for granted." Blair glared at the other woman. "At least you have an alibi now. I'm sure you two were together the night of Skylar's murder. I hope you're happy now." She turned around to leave.

"I don't want her. I want you." Grant grabbed her arm to stop her.

Nolan fired off several more shots.

"Who is this guy, anyway?" Grant glared at Nolan.

"You of all people should recognize tabloid trash when you see it." Chelsea sneered at Grant. "You're not so great, Grant. I knew you when you were nobody. Just because you're famous now, doesn't mean you're better than the rest of us. And for the record, I no longer want you, either." She wrapped the sheet around herself and headed into the bathroom.

"You won't get away with this." Grant took a menacing step toward Nolan in a threatening move. "Give me that camera."

Nolan took a step back. "Back off, Kingsley."

Grant pulled a switchblade out of his jeans' pocket. "I said turn it over, Nolan. You didn't ask to take my picture, so you don't own the rights to those pictures. You can't prove anything without them."

I jumped to my feet, with Jaz right beside me.

Blair screamed.

Grant stumbled back a step.

Nolan's flash shuttered out of reflex.

"How about with a couple witnesses?" I said. "The gig's up, Grant. We saw the whole thing."

"Heard it, too," Jaz said, the stars dimming quickly from her eyes. "Interesting choice of weapon. I take it you like sharp objects."

"Whoa, you've got me all wrong." Grant started backing away, waving his hands in front of him. "I'm a lover, not a fighter. I wouldn't hurt anyone."

"Says the man with a knife," Nolan said.

"And another woman in his bed," Blair added.

"The facts don't look good," I pointed out.

"I want to talk to my lawyer." Grant pulled out his phone.

"Now that's the first smart thing you've said since you'll definitely be hearing from mine." Blair grabbed Nolan's arm. "Come on, Nolan. I've got a husband to sue."

15

What a day, I thought late that afternoon, as I tooled around my house with my hard hat on, inspecting the latest renovations. Nik had done the initial work, but we'd decided to renovate even more that was out of his scope of capabilities.

The place was really coming along. We'd had a couple more walls knocked down, going with an open concept floorplan. We had guest bedrooms and a bathroom upstairs and decided to use my bedroom and bathroom as the master suite since it was bigger, and Nik's bedroom as an office. His bathroom wasn't attached to his bedroom, so it would just be a main downstairs bathroom for everyone, and we got rid of his kitchen, adding the extra room to one big open great room.

Heading over to the kitchen area, I took my hard hat off and stopped short. A miniature version of the iconic Bellagio fountain sat in the middle of our table. I didn't see a cord, so it had to be battery operated. I pushed a button, and a choreographed water display set to Greek music and red and white Marti lights went off.

There were no words anymore.

I slapped my forehead and poured a glass of chardonnay as I started dinner. I looked in the refrigerator and decided to make Souvlaki. I had meat thawed out, so I took a moment to season the meat and then cut it into chunks to grill and make skewers out of. Once I had it prepared, I slid the plate onto the warmer. Next, I put together a Greek salad with tomatoes, cucumbers, feta cheese, olives, and a drizzle of olive oil. Then for dessert we would have Greek yogurt with honey and walnuts.

Setting the table, I took my seat just as Nik walked through the front door. He slipped off his jacket, slid out of his holster, pulled off his tie, then joined me in the kitchen. First thing he did was wash his hands thoroughly.

"Hi." I smiled.

"Hi." He winked.

Leaning down, he gave me a kiss, and I handed him a beer before he took a seat. "What a day," he said.

"Funny you should say that. I was just thinking the same thing." I joined him.

"You first." He narrowed his eyes and took a sip of his beer. "What have you been up to, Ballas?"

"Nothing you didn't already know about, Detective. Jaz and I put up more flyers like we said we were going to. We just broadened our search a little." I took a bite of a meat skewer because I knew he was going to ask for details.

And he wouldn't like them.

"Like where?" He dug into his salad.

I pointed to my full mouth and made him wait while I finished chewing, wondering if I was going to hurt my jaw from being overworked as I formulated my answer. "Okay, fine, we went to Lakeshore

Heights," I finally said on a sigh, having no other choice, then rubbed my aching jaw.

"What?" His featured went from shock to fear to anger and frustration. "This is why I don't want you involved in *any* investigation. That place is shady. All sorts of things happen out there, Ballas. Besides, it's not even our jurisdiction. It crosses the town line."

"It was daylight. We were never in any real danger. I know it crosses the town line, but maybe the puppies have left town as well. It also backs up to a lake and the woods. After our pets ended up in the woods, I figured it might be smart to see if anyone had seen twenty-two puppies and two full-sized poodles."

He sighed. "I know you both want to find those dogs desperately. We all do. I also know you want your aunt's name cleared. I'm just worried with a dog-napper and a killer still on the loose, not to mention counterfeit money still circulating." He pinched the bridge of his nose then took another drink of his beer before asking, "Well, any luck?"

"I know you're worried, and I'm sorry. I'm really not trying to worry you." I squeezed his hand. "I'm just trying to help." I took a sip of chardonnay before telling him the rest. "We didn't have luck with puppies, but we definitely saw shady."

"What exactly does that mean?" He locked eyes with mine and held my gaze. "Or do I want to know?"

I chewed my bottom lip. "Let's just say we can rule Chelsea Turner and Grant Kingsley out as suspects in Skylar's murder."

Nik drew his brows together. "How so?"

"They are definitely each other's alibi's. While Jaz and I were down by the water, Blair showed up with that guy Nolan."

"Really?" Nik's brows shot up. "Was Grant with them?"

"Oh, he was there, all right, but he was definitely not *with* them." I shook my head. "He was with Chelsea Turner...in bed."

Nik paused with his fork halfway to his mouth. "Wait, then why was Nolan there with Blair?"

"Because he's paparazzi. He's been in town trying to get the scoop on Grant Kingsley. Grant had been keeping Blair and the kids at the Clearview Hotel with their nanny, under the guise of protecting them from a killer on the loose. Really, he just didn't want to get caught hooking up with an old flame from high school."

Nik whistled. "I bet Blair wasn't too happy about that."

"She said she wanted a divorce. I can't say that I blame her." I finished my salad. "Chelsea was angry because she said Grant told her he was going to leave his wife for her, and she actually believed him."

"What did Grant do in all of this?" Nik finished his meat skewer.

I shrugged as I took our desserts out of the refrigerator and put them in front of us, hoping to soften the blow with something sweet. "He pulled out a knife and threatened Nolan if he didn't give him the camera."

Nik choked on his food. After taking a swig of beer he gaped at me. "A knife? Why didn't you call me immediately?"

"Because I had it handled. Grant's not a killer. Jaz and I had the element of surprise. We were hiding in the bushes—"

"Of course, you were."

"—and when we jumped out at him, he backed

right down and dropped the knife. Blair threatened divorce, and Grant called his lawyer. End of story." I took a bite of my yogurt honey nut dessert. "But enough about me. Your turn."

"You're gonna be the death of me yet, Ballas." Nik rubbed his temple and snorted. "My day wasn't nearly as dangerous as yours, but it might have been even more dramatic. Boomer and I inspected the sugar shanty first. Someone had definitely been living there for a while, but they're long gone now. The fur doesn't look like dog fur. I'm thinking the person was homeless and living off the land. It's been known to happen before, but not in a while."

My face fell. "So, no puppies?"

His gaze softened. "I'm afraid not."

I tipped my head to the side and studied him curiously. "What took you so long getting home?"

"We got a domestic disturbance call." Nik polished off his dessert with a moan of pleasure.

My eyes widened. "Domestic disturbance? Really?"

"The neighbor of Ursula Smith's Airbnb called because she heard fighting and a couple loud bangs coming from next door. When we got there, we found Ursula's girlfriend, Tammy, shouting, and Drake Fontana slamming pots and pans around the kitchen. The man really does have a temper."

"I don't get that trio. They obviously don't like each other."

"You would be right about that. Tammy accused Ursula of having an affair with Drake. Ursula finally came clean that all the sneaking around they'd been doing was Drake giving Ursula cooking lessons."

I snapped my fingers, remembering. "Wait, is that what he was helping her with before when she said he screwed up and she wasn't going to take the fall alone?"

"Apparently, Drake tried out his new recipes by preparing a special dinner for Tammy. Ursula lied and pretended she cooked the meal because she wanted to impress her girlfriend and then propose. But Drake changed the planned menu, making food Tammy couldn't eat, which made her feel like Ursula didn't really know her at all. So as a consolation, Drake offered to teach Ursula how to cook so she could prepare the meal herself and get it right this time, but Tammy suspected they were having an affair."

"What happened?"

"Ursula came clean, and Tammy was so moved, she said yes on the spot."

"You win. Your day was definitely more dramatic than mine."

"And definitely less dangerous." He pointed at me. "Let's hope tomorrow is better because my heart can't take much more."

∽

THE NEXT MORNING I was on my way into work, but I had to stop by Clearview National Bank first. I had to get a certified check for Ronald Banks of Banks Construction. Ronald was doing our remodel.

Nik wasn't a fan of his ever since I investigated a case at the Senior Single's Club in the back of Rosalita's Restaurant. Ronald had thought I was looking for a man, even though I was hardly a senior. He was a short, stocky, bald man in his fifties, but he looked much older from his years spent working in the sun.

Ronald was harmless.

Now that Nik and I were moving in together,

Ronald was finally taking the hint that I was off the market for real. Clearview was a small town, and Banks Construction was the best in the business. I finished my transaction and on my way outside, I saw Dino Willis. He turned my way and I smiled, giving him a little wave. He quickly waved back and then turned away...

But not before I saw the black eye he was sporting.

I frowned, wondering if there was more than trouble in paradise between Raven and him. She *had* looked angry after he'd had words with Hannah the other day, even though Hannah was quite a bit older than him, but who was I to judge. I just hoped he was okay and would speak out if he wasn't.

I stepped outside to wait for Ronald in the parking lot. It was a beautiful day. The sun was shining, and the temperature was warming up quickly. A spring breeze carried the smell of cut grass and flowers to my nose.

I glanced at my watch. Where was Ronald?

Just then Dino came walking out of the bank and bumped smack into me because he was looking down at his phone texting someone.

"Whoops, easy there." I stumbled then caught my balance.

He looked up in surprise. "Sorry, Kalli. I didn't see you there." He pushed his glasses up his nose and winced.

"That's quite the shiner." I studied his swollen eye that was different shades of purple, gray, and black. "Are you okay?"

He shrugged. "I'm fine. Just a klutz."

"Let me guess. You ran into a door," I teased.

"Something like that." He cleared his throat.

I touched his arm. "How's Raven? She didn't get hurt, did she?"

He blinked, then frowned. *Last I checked, there's not much that can hurt an ex-MMA fighter.* He cleared his throat and stepped out of my reach. "She's good. Well, I better get to work. Don't want to leave it all for Milly to handle." He tipped his head at me and then walked away at a brisk pace.

He pulled out of the parking lot...but didn't head in the direction of the daycare.

Very strange. Oh, well. Maybe he had another errand to run first. I spotted Ronald as he pulled into the parking lot right after Dino left. I waved, and Ronald came to a stop by the curb then rolled down his window.

"Hey, Ms. Ballas, how are you this fine morning?" Ronald was on his best behavior, given my boyfriend was a detective.

"I'm great, Mr. Banks. Hope you're doing well." I handed him the certified bank check. "This should cover what you've done so far."

He eyed the check with a smile. "This will do just fine." He folded the check in half and slipped it into his pocket. "It won't be much longer now before we're finished. I bet you and Detective Stevens will be glad to have us out of your hair."

"Nik is pretty handy, but this job called for a professional. I'm just glad he finally agreed to let you guys help and that you guys could squeeze us in. I know how busy this time of year can be in the construction business."

"Your family and the detective's family have given me lots of business over the years. It was my pleasure to help you both out." He chuckled. "Besides, you did quite a number on that wall with your sledgehammer."

"Apparently, I thought I was handier than I am." I laughed. "Well, thanks again, Ronald. I really do appreciate it."

"You're very welcome, Kalli." He saluted me. "Well, guess I better get to it, then." He gave me a wave, as he put his truck in gear and pulled away from the curb.

I hurried along as well and got to Full Disclosure in record time.

I had a final fitting with Maria for her wedding trousseau, and I had a handful of sketches to show Kosmos for Winnie's anniversary gift. When I walked through the front door, Clayton was browsing my Kalli Originals stand. I stifled a gasp and ducked behind a clothing rack as he glanced toward the front door.

There was no way I would design lingerie for my aunt for *any* of her suitors.

I managed to skirt the edge of the store until I reached the stairs leading to my loft. I slipped up the stairs without anyone the wiser, thank goodness. A little while later, Jaz sent Maria up to try on her trousseau. I had a changing screen set up in one corner for my customers to discreetly try on original commissions. And we were so high up, no one could see them when they came out in front of the mirror.

"It's fabulous, Kalli. I can't thank you enough." She eyed herself from every direction. "I feel beautiful."

"You look gorgeous. Sully is going to love it."

"Yay." She clapped her hands. "The day is going to be here before you know it." She went back behind the screen to change. "Can I take these with me?" she asked as she carried them out with her.

"Absolutely." I nodded, wrapping her lingerie up

carefully. "You're all set. You can settle up with Jaz down below."

"Wonderful. Have a fabulous day."

"Same to you." I barely finished my morning tea when Kosmos came up the stairs. "Right on time, cousin."

"Of course. I'm not Silas." He grunted, then sanitized his hands as he looked around warily. "Do I, um, enter?"

I laughed. "It's just lingerie, Kos."

"I don't know anything about all this stuff." His face flushed beat red. "I mean I *know* about it, and er um, how it works and all that, but I don't know what a woman like Winnie might like."

"Lucky for you, I do." I pulled out my book of designs and flipped to a spot tabbed Winnie. I set the book on a table before him. I always designed three or four ideas to give my commissioned customers choices.

His eyes widened and then misted over with so much love. "These are beautiful, Kalli. You really have a gift."

"Awe, thank you. That means a lot."

He stared at the designs in wonder. "It's like you captured who she is as a person. Her essence. What she's like as a woman. How do you do that?"

I shrugged. "A woman is a lot more than her outward appearance. I get to know who she is on the inside and try to match both in my designs."

"Well, you've succeeded." He gave me a quick hug which was rare for him. "I'll take them all."

I giggled. "Okay, then. I have a good eye. I can usually get pretty close to a woman's measurements just by looking at her. I'll sew the lingerie, and after you surprise her, I can do any alterations she might need for her special weekend."

"Special weekend?"

"Kosmos, really?" I laughed. "I certainly hope you're whisking her away someplace romantic after all this."

"Right. Right. Good idea. You're a lifesaver, Kalli."

"I know." I winked. "Better hurry before everything books up."

He was gone in a flash.

I came down for a lunch break to join Jaz. "Busy morning."

"Same for me." She shook her head, and then smiled with curiosity in her eyes. "Your cousin sure flew out of here in a hurry."

"The man was so focused on getting the perfect anniversary present, he forgot all about making any anniversary plans."

"Men." She laughed.

"Amen." I joined her.

We both grabbed our lunch from the refrigerator in the break room and sat at the table, choosing to eat in today.

"Speaking of men," I said. "I ran into Dino this morning at the bank. He had a massive black eye."

"I saw that last night. After we left Lakeshore Heights, I drove home. I saw his car parked at the pawnshop and slowed down to offer my help, but the expression on his face showed his embarrassment when I saw his eye, so I just waved and kept going. He was unloading a bunch of electronics. I hope he's not hurting for money."

"Interesting. He literally just deposited a duffel bag full of money this morning. I thought it was income from the daycare. Maybe it was from all the stuff he pawned instead."

"Why the black eye?"

"I asked him about it. He said he and Raven were fine, and that he was just a klutz. I heard his thoughts. Raven used to be an MMA fighter. I didn't see that one coming. She seems like one interesting woman."

"She sure does. Interesting and mysterious." Jaz looked me in the eye. "You thinking what I'm thinking?"

"Maybe it's time we got to know Raven Monroe."

16

That afternoon I got a tip that Raven had an appointment at my aunt's salon today. Apparently, she had booked a deep tissue massage by Perry in the back and told the masseuse she'd overworked her muscles. I decided to wait until she was finished, and then see if I could talk with her. I didn't know her, but from what I'd observed, she seemed a little high strung. Maybe if she was relaxed, she would be more open to a conversation.

Dino was a friend, and I was really worried about him.

Meanwhile, Mayor Zimmerman was getting her short, sophisticated, gray streaked hairdo touched up. She always looked perfectly put together.

"Afternoon, Mayor." I smiled as I ran a sanitized wipe over a seat in the waiting room close to the salon chair she sat in. One of my aunt's new hair stylists, Billy Rae, trimmed the mayor's hair.

"Good afternoon, Ms. Ballas." The mayor's face remained smile free, and her indigo eyes were glued to mine. "I'm not foolish enough to believe you're doing as you were told and staying out of Sklyar Delaney's murder investigation. Please tell me you're here to inform me of a break in the case?"

Billy Rae let out a little squeak, and her hand slipped. "Sorry," she quickly said when the mayor eyed her sharp scissors. She shook back her blond ponytail with a deep breath. "The thought of some crazed killer running around Clearview in plain sight, and we have no idea who it is, terrifies me."

"You can rest assured; we're doing everything we can to keep the streets safe." The mayor eyed Billy Rae warily. "You sure you know what you're doing? My appointment was with Tasoula, but apparently, she has better things to do than tend to her business."

"Oh, don't you worry none about that. I graduated top of my class in cosmetology school just one month ago today." Billy Rae beamed.

The mayor's eyes bulged, and her mouth parted but no words came out.

"Impressive, I know." Billy Rae snapped her gum, and it almost fell out into the mayor's hair. Billy's eyes widened then she swallowed it before continuing. "Anyway, Ms. Tasoula is late on account of her big date tonight."

"You don't say." The mayor's jaw hardened.

"Them Dupont brothers, Antoine and Louise, are just so sweet. They're getting a surprise picnic ready for Tasoula. They told her to meet them here for a surprise at closing, but they didn't say what. They asked for access to the back room to get things ready, but I made them spill the beans first."

"Imagine that." The mayor's silver brow arched high.

"I know, isn't it so romantic?" Billy Rae giggled.

"It's something." The mayor looked at me then raised a brow. "You okay?"

I closed my gaping mouth. "No, I'm not okay." I looked at Billy Rae. "You didn't let the men in the back room, did you?"

"Course not. I just wanted them to spill the tea, but my mama didn't raise no fool." She beamed. "I told them they had to make their preparations elsewhere, but that I would pass the message on to Miss Tasoula to meet them back here for a surprise at closing."

I let out a sigh of relief. I didn't trust those brothers one bit.

"Back to you, Ms. Ballas," the mayor said. "I pray you have better news for me than your detective has lately. More counterfeit bills showed up at the bank just yesterday. There's been no luck in finding the puppy-nappers. People are afraid to walk the streets with their pets. And we still haven't caught the killer."

Billy Rae shuddered, and her scissors jerked.

The mayor eyed Billy Rae carefully then leaned away as she spoke to me. "I need this case wrapped up before the summer festivals start. This town counts on the revenue from the festivals, and the spring festival came up short with everything that's been going on. People don't want to come to Clearview if they're afraid. And if they don't come, then they don't spend money. Please tell me something else has happened that I don't know about?"

Well, Drake lied about cooking for Ursula's girlfriend and then giving Ursula cooking lessons. And Grant cheated on his wife by having an affair with Chelsea. Oh, and Nolan is the paparazzi, I thought, and muttered, "Liar and cheaters and lowlifes, oh my."

"English please. You're starting to sound like your mother and aunt," the mayor said dryly. "What in the world does that all mean?"

I blinked and cleared my mind. "Basically, that they alibied out."

"All you're doing is ruling suspects out." She huffed out a frustrated breath. "How are we supposed to close a case if we don't have anyone left to arrest?"

"Ruling suspects out is one step closer to finding the real killer," I said logically with a calm tone. The mayor was usually so level-headed. If she lost it, what chance did the rest of us have? I wanted this case wrapped up even more than she did because that meant clearing my aunt's name, but not at the expense of putting the wrong person behind bars.

Just then Raven came out from the massage room.

"Excuse me, mayor." I stood. "If I hear anything else, you'll be the first to know. I really have to go now. There's someone I need to speak with." I hurried after Raven as she walked out the salon's door.

She walked for several yards as I tried to catch up to her, then she suddenly stopped short and turned around to face me with a guarded expression on her face. She tucked her black and brown streaked hair behind her ear and then touched her choke collar with her short, black painted fingernails. "Are you following me?"

I blinked. "Um, no, yes, I mean I would like to speak with you for a moment if you have the time. I'm Kalli Ballas." I held out my hand.

She reached out warily to shake my hand. "I know who you are." *The question is what do you want with me? How much do you know?* She dropped her hand and flexed it a couple of times as if it were sore. "How can I help you?"

I squirted some lotion into my hands. It had hand sanitizer in it, but she didn't have to know that. I was trying out new ways to disguise my quirks so I wouldn't throw people off. "You're dating Dino Willis, right?"

She narrowed her eyes, making me wonder if she really was the jealous sort. "What's this about?"

I looked her over, and she seemed completely unharmed. Vibrant even. "I'm so glad you seem to be okay."

Her posture stiffened. "Why wouldn't I be?"

"I saw Dino at the bank this morning, and his eye looks terrible." I winced. "What happened to him?"

She relaxed a little. "What did he say happened?"

"He said he's a klutz. And that he sort of ran into a wall." I held up my hands. "That must be some wall."

She shrugged. "I wasn't with him at the time. If he said he ran into a wall, then he ran into a wall."

"It looks bad." I crossed my arms. "I'm worried about him. Did he have it checked out by a doctor?"

"It's just a bruise. Small capillaries near the skin's surface broke and leaked red blood cells that pooled beneath the skin causing discoloration," she rambled off as if talking about bruises and recovery were second nature to her. "All a doctor would do is advise him to R.I.C.E."

"Excuse me?" I arched an eyebrow high.

She blinked as if just realizing she'd spoken all that out loud. Sorry. She shrugged and explained, "Rest, ice, compression, and elevation to reduce swelling and speed up healing. I told him to apply a cold compress right away to constrict the blood vessels. There's nothing more to do except wait it out."

"I thought you weren't with him when it happened."

Her jaw hardened a smidge. "I wasn't. I meant when I saw him later."

"Right." I nodded and paused a beat. "I suppose you *would* know all about bruises and healing."

She was immediately wary again. "What makes you say so?"

I shrugged. "Your former fighting days."

She crossed her arms over her chest and raised her chin a notch. "I never told anyone except Dino about that, and I'm pretty sure he wouldn't say anything to anyone, especially since I asked him not to."

Whoops. "He must have let it slip, or maybe I heard it somewhere else." I studied her body language. "What's the big deal? I think it's kind of cool. Why don't you want anyone to know?"

"Do you want everyone to know all of *your* secrets?" She looked at me as if she could see straight into my soul.

For a brief moment, I wondered if she could read minds, too, but then realized I was letting my imagination run away with me. I laughed a little too loud before responding, "I guess not."

She glanced at her watch and cursed under her breath, but I heard it. "Look, if there's nothing else I can help you with, I have to go. I'm running late for an appointment." She started walking away.

"Appointment for what?" I called after her retreating back. "What do you do for a living now?"

She didn't answer. For a moment, I wondered if she even heard me, but then her pace picked up until she disappeared around a corner as if she were on a mission. What I wouldn't give to know what that mission entailed...

Something told me she wouldn't be so nice if she caught me following her again.

Jaz and I picked up takeout from Rosalita's and brought it to the station for dinner. Lately, we'd been doing everything together, just like old times, since our men were busy working the cases: counterfeit money, puppy-napping, and murder.

"That smells amazing, Ballas." Nik looked up and smiled his appreciation, his eyes softening when they met mine.

I set the food containers down on the table he and Boomer sat at, comparing notes. Behind them was a Smartboard full of details and pinned up pictures about the cases. They called this room the war room. There were files and papers everywhere, but they swore they knew where everything was and not to touch their organized chaos. No worries there.

Zeus only knew what germs lurked in the middle of that mess.

"Babe, you're a goddess." Boomer jumped up and swung a giggling Jaz in a circle then set her down all wobbling with dizziness as he dove into the Mexican food. His eyes rolled back, and he moaned his pleasure.

Not much beat Rosalita's enchiladas.

Jaz and I took our seats across from the men at the table and dished out plates for ourselves as well. We all took a moment of silence to enjoy our dinner. Great food with ones you loved without having to cook was the best.

"The mayor is getting frustrated," I finally said.

Nik paused. "I know, but how do *you* know?"

I wiped my mouth and took a sip of iced tea before responding. "I ran into her at Hera's Halo this afternoon."

"Captain Crenshaw has been coming down hard on us to at least wrap up something." Boomer shook his head. "It's not like we're not trying. All we've been doing is working on these cases. Too many things are happening at once without enough manpower. Every time we take one step forward, something sets us two steps back."

"I'm sorry, babe." Jaz walked around behind Boomer and massaged his shoulders, and he moaned even louder than over the food. Her brow puckered. "What happened this time?"

"I thought we were getting somewhere with the Coopers and the sugar shanty," he said between groans. "But then the shanty turned out to be nothing more than a homeless person taking shelter, but they're long gone now. And then today the Coopers came in and reported their dogs were missing."

"What?" Jaz's hands froze.

"I know." Boomer reached his hand back and pulled her around onto his lap and hugged her. "I'm sorry to say this, but it's highly unlikely they're the puppy-nappers if their own dogs and their papers have gone missing."

She sighed. "I'm sure you're right."

"And their dogs are purebreds," Nik pointed out, "so they're definitely worth something to a buyer looking to make a buck in the show ring or even the puppy mill ring. With papers and points in the ring, those dogs will definitely fetch a good price."

"So, what now?" I asked.

"Now, we add that to our growing list of things to investigate." Nik rubbed his forehead. "No pressure."

I reached out and squeezed his hand. "You've got this. I believe in you."

He winked. "Thanks, Ballas."

Suddenly, we heard voices raised out in the hall.

Nik and Boomer stood, and Jaz returned to her

seat. Before the men could move any further, Tate burst through the door with Aunt Tasoula slung over his shoulder in a sparkling evening gown worthy of a Miss USA pageant.

"Put me down, you tree trunk." Aunt Tasoula pummeled her fists on Tate's back, to no avail.

He gently set her down even though his expression was pure frustration and anger. "Lock her up."

"On what charge?" I asked.

"This woman says she doesn't want me, but then she proceeds to be a meddling menace when it comes to my love life."

"Me?" Aunt Tasoula shoved her lopsided updo back in place and pulled up one long white satin glove that had slipped down to her wrist. "I on two-on-one picnic under the stars date with my boo-boos to decide if I give batons—"

"Boo-boos are an injury. I think you mean your boos," Jaz clarified. "Or your baes."

"What a bae?" My aunt's face scrunched up.

"Before anyone else."

"Yes. I have two boo-boo babies, but they no before anyone else. Family come first." Aunt Tasoula swiped her hand through the air. "I no keep up with the jingle."

"Lingo?" I asked.

"Who he? I no have room for three." My aunt rubbed her temple. "Never mind that. Okay? Okay. So, this Viking storm in and carry me off."

"Isn't that what you wanted?" I asked carefully.

"You did?" Tate scratched his head, staring at my aunt.

"No." Aunt Tasoula crossed her arms under her chest and looked away.

"Why not?" Jaz appeared just as confused as I was.

"He yell at me." My aunt fanned her face as if she were about to faint.

"First, you threaten Skylar, and she winds up dead in your shop," Tate spoke carefully. "Then you parade around a man much older than you. Just when I think you've moved on with him, you start whacking him on the head with your baton. Next, you date two men at once who I'm pretty sure are quite a few years younger than you. So again, I think you've moved on. Just when I'm ready to let you go and move on myself, my date disappears."

"What do you mean, disappears?" I looked at Nik.

"I was supposed to have a date of my own tonight, but when I went to pick up Hannah at her sister's house, Helen said she was gone. She said Hannah had a few things to take care of, but she should have been back hours ago. She never showed up, and I think *this* one had something to do with it." Tate pointed his finger at Aunt Tasoula.

"He crazy Viking. And dangerous. Lock *him* up." Aunt Tasoula harrumphed. "What I want with a Hannah Banana?"

"Look, no one is getting locked up." Nik blew out a breath. "Have a seat and start from the beginning."

"I'll put on a pot of coffee." Boomer headed over to the barista station. "I have a feeling this is going to be a long night."

"Why don't you ladies go home." Nik looked at Jaz and me.

"Oh, we're not going anywhere," Jaz and I said simultaneously, and settled in for the show.

17

"Aunt Tasoula, are you here?" I knocked on the door of Hera's Halo the next morning. "I have your baked goods from Ma."

The salon wasn't open yet, but Ma said my aunt had called in an early morning order of Baklava. It was a sweet pastry loaf made of layers of phyllo dough, filled with chopped nuts and sweetened with honey. She also ordered Loukoumades, which are deep-fried dough balls drizzled with honey and sprinkled with cinnamon or powdered sugar. Ma figured she must be hosting a party for her customers.

Last night my aunt had told how the Dupont brothers had changed their surprise picnic at her salon to one under the stars at the park. Just when they were getting to the good part, Tate had come running out of the woods like Big Foot, yelling and scaring her Frenchies until they were frozen. They didn't make a move as Sasquatch threw her over his shoulder and stormed off, demanding to know what she had done with his Hannah Banana.

While Tate claimed she kept yelling, *Sick him*, trying to get her bulldogs to give chase and nip his heels, but the cowards didn't so much as wag a tail in his direction. So, he carried her off to put her in a cage where she belonged, but Nik and Boomer let them both go. Tate left to continue to search for Hannah, while Aunt Tasoula had obviously made other plans.

Speaking of my aunt, she finally hurried over to the door and unlocked it.

I blinked.

My aunt wore a deep red satin pajama set and high heeled slippers with feathers on the toes. She'd added long silky extensions to her hair and had a face full of makeup on. She held out her hands and wiggled her red and white striped fingernails at me.

"Here's your order." I handed her the boxes and looked around the empty salon. "Are you having a pajama party for your guests?"

"Pajama party, yes." She leaned forward and whispered. "Party for two."

"Two?" I peeked past her but still didn't see anyone. "Clayton surprise me with special date in my private lounge in back. One-on-one time with me. Slumber party better than picnic. Maybe he get baton...maybe no." She winked. "Time will tell. Bye bye. I go now." She closed the door in my face, locked it, and pulled down the shade.

Nik should have locked her up for her own good.

Next stop, I was delivering the Baklava I'd promised to Gary at the Clearview Motel. Ma had agreed to make him some after I made her think it was her idea. She just loved to spoil people she liked. And since she didn't consider what I did as a *real* job, she always called on me to deliver things for her when her regular crew was busy delivering actual purchased items.

I didn't mind. I enjoyed visiting with Gary. I enjoyed visiting with my aunt as well, when she wasn't crazy. I suddenly got the strongest sensation that someone was behind me again. Whipping around, I raised my hands in a ready position to defend myself like I'd been taught, but no one was there. My gaze darted everywhere, and I could have sworn I saw a flash of something, but then it was gone.

The parking lot was deserted other than a stray cat that hissed before running around my aunt's salon. Maybe that was what I had sensed. Shaking off the chills, I hopped in my car and realized I'd left it unlocked. That wasn't like me. I could have sworn I'd locked it. Quickly scanning the back seat to make sure I was alone, I started my Prius and locked the doors before heading to the outskirts of town.

It felt like it took forever to get there. I kept checking my rear-view mirror, but I didn't see anyone behind me. My imagination must be working on overdrive. Finally, I saw the Clearview Motel. With a sigh of relief, I pulled into the parking lot of the Motel and was surprised to see Nik's car there.

I walked through the front door into the lobby. Nik sat on a chair facing a couch the Dupont brothers sat on. He had his notebook out, so I assumed he was questioning them about something. I walked over to Gary, who stood behind the front desk, and handed him the Baklava.

Nik's gaze met mine. He was always aware of his surroundings. He arched a suspicious brow at seeing me there, so I pointed to the dessert and held up my hands innocently. He shook his head and went back to questioning the brothers.

"Thanks, Kalli. Lisa will be so happy. This is her absolute favorite dessert. Your mother is a queen." Gary smelled the dessert and sighed in pleasure as his eyes closed and his lips tipped up in a smile of bliss.

"And I am her worker bee."

"Well, I certainly appreciate you coming out here, brightening my day." His glance shot over to the sitting area. "It's been quite a morning."

"I can see that." Nik's face remained unreadable as the brothers talked and he wrote notes in his notebook. "What's going on?"

"Antoine and Louis came back last night to find their room broken into." Gary shook his head. "Someone knew exactly where the camera was in the hall and sprayed black paint over it, then broke the lock to the room and trashed the place. It's strange because they didn't take anything of value."

I frowned and glanced over at the brothers. They moved their hands rapidly as they talked, as if they were frustrated, but they didn't seem as upset as I would think they would be after having their personal space invaded. I would be terrified, but then again, maybe that was just me.

I thought about the situation. "Sounds like the person who broke in was looking for something specific."

Gary was already nodding. "That was your detective's thought as well. He's been questioning them for the last hour."

Vicky walked into the lobby from down the hall, sliding a screwdriver back into her toolbelt. "Locks are all changed, Gary. The camera in the hall is fixed as well. Anything else you need me to do before I go?"

"Thanks, Vicky." Gary handed her a check. "I appreciate you coming on such short notice. We should be good now, barring no other catastrophes happen. There must be a full moon or something. Everyone's gone crazy."

"I was just telling Jaz that the other day." I thought of my aunt.

Vicky looked at me as if just now realizing I was there. "Hey, Kalli. How are you?"

"It's like Gary said. Life is crazy at the moment. I'm delivering Ma's goodies this morning before heading into work. I saw Jasper earlier at Aphrodite's. He's still working on the patio for Pop."

"That's where I'm headed now." Vicky leaned over conspiratorially and lowered her voice as she touched my arm. "Between you and me, he can use all the help he can get." *That one's a mystery I'm still working out. Hopefully, I'll succeed before I move on to the next job.* She winked and let go of my arm.

My heart pinged, and I gasped. "You're leaving?"

"Yes." She looked at me strangely. "I'm headed to Aphrodite's to help Jasper, remember?"

Whoops. "Yes, that's right. Like I said...crazy." I twirled my finger around my head like I'd lost my mind.

"Stay away. It seems to be contagious." Vicky laughed. "Well, guess I'd better go." She waved and walked out the lobby door.

I wondered when she would walk out of Clearview for good...and why. I had thought she'd moved here permanently. I bet if the mamas knew, they never would have tried to fix Jasper up with her.

I grabbed my backpack and headed for the front door.

"Not so fast, Ballas," a male voice said from behind me.

I winced then pasted on a smile and turned around, forcing enthusiasm into my voice. "Detective, fancy seeing you here."

He narrowed his eyes. "I could say the same thing."

I threw up my hands and gave up the act. "I'm telling you; I had no idea about the break-in. I was making deliveries for Ma. That's all."

"I believe you." He relaxed and rolled his head on his shoulders. "So much for good luck from all those Martis bracelets. Clearview has had nothing but a string of bad luck since the 40th high school reunion. I'm beginning to wonder if things will ever turn around."

Nik's cell phone rang, and he looked at me as he answered."Detective Stevens here." He listened, and the frown lines deepened in his forehead. "Roger that. I'll be right there." He hung up.

"What's wrong now?"

"Nolan Ryder is at the news station, reporting live. He was supposed to have an interview with Grant Kingsley and Chelsey Turner, but that got canceled."

"How is that newsworthy?"

Nik's intense gaze met mine. "Because Grant Kingsley was jumped and is in the hospital, Chelsey Turner checked out of Lakeshore Heights and skipped town, and, according to the nanny, Blair Kingsley is missing."

FORGET WORK. I tagged along with Nik to the hospital and then the news station and finally the police station where he was to brief the captain and the mayor. For once, he didn't try to stop me.

"Where are we at, Detective Stevens?" Captain Crenshaw paced the war room, stopping to look over the Smartboard.

"Grant said the nanny was with the kids while he was out with Blair this morning, trying to patch up their marriage. Someone jumped him and he ended up unconscious in the hospital. When he came to, he discovered his nanny had reported his wife missing." Nik looked at the Smartboard as well. "I was there for over an hour. Before I left, a call came in. It was a disguised voice, asking for a hefty ransom from Grant if he wanted his wife back."

"Be ready to trace the call if the kidnapper calls back, Detective," Captain Crenshaw said with intensity.

"I'm on it." Nik made a note.

"How about you, Detective Matheson?" The captain looked at Boomer, the lines in his forehead deeper than normal. All these investigations were clearly taking their toll on him, and Mayor Zimmerman breathing down his neck didn't help. Good thing Chloe understood and was giving him space. He had been through a divorce, and so had she. That was one of the reasons why they were so good together.

"I checked out Lakeshore Heights and the front desk manager, Arnold, said Chelsea Turner had just checked out that morning." Boomer flipped through the pages of his notebook. "I radioed the patrol cars with information on her, as well as her car, and passed it on to our neighboring law enforcement agencies, but so far, no luck. She must be hiding out somewhere because we have connections all over the place. If someone spotted her, they would let us know immediately."

"Or she's the one who has Blair Kingsley." Mayor Zimmerman worked through her thoughts out loud. "Jealousy can make people do crazy things they might not normally do. Ms. Turner was pretty angry when Grant refused to leave his wife for her, so maybe she figured she would get back at him by kidnapping his wife."

"Chelsea doesn't strike me as a murderer," I mused.

"Maybe not a murderer, but she might be capable of kidnapping," the mayor countered. "She might intend on returning Blair unharmed, but she also might feel Grant owes her something for what he put her through. Being a flight attendant, she could have him wire her money, and then skip town fairly easily to pretty much anywhere."

"What about Hannah Schwartz?" the captain asked. "Last I checked, she was still missing, correct?"

"That would be correct," Nik confirmed. "Tate hasn't heard a word from her, and her sister Helen said she hasn't either."

"Do you think Hannah's disappearance is connected to Blair's?" Boomer studied the smart board and his notes.

"I don't think so." Nik shook his head. "Blair has no connection to Hannah that I know of, so I don't see how they could be linked."

"What about Tasoula?" The mayor eyed me. "She certainly had reason for wanting Hannah to disappear, same that she wanted Skylar out of the picture. Seems to me she's still our number one suspect for a couple of cases."

"I can vouch that my aunt was preoccupied with the Dupont brothers when Hannah went missing." I sat up straighter. "Same with Clayton this morning when Blair went missing."

"What was she doing?" The mayor quirked a brow.

"Being the Majorette and handing out batons." I raised my hands, palms up.

"I won't pretend to know what that means." The

captain sighed. "A lot of your aunt's actions are questionable, but I doubt she's a killer."

"Anyone is capable of violence if pushed hard enough." The mayor stared the captain down.

"Look, I know you want these cases wrapped up." He stared back. "We all do. But last I heard; people were innocent until proven guilty. I won't have these investigations rushed just for the sake of closing cases." A muscle in his jaw flexed.

"This town doesn't need people who are afraid to do their jobs." Her lips pursed into a thin flat line.

Silence filled the room with tension.

The captain's cell phone rang, and we all jumped. He left to answer it, and the mayor headed to her own office, clearly frustrated and in a bad mood. Nik and Boomer went back to discussing their notes and the smart board.

I stood and gathered my backpack then headed toward the door. "See you later, Detective. I'm going into work for a little while."

He waved distractedly, so I left and went to the parking lot.

A light drizzle had started, so I hurried my steps to my car. That weird sensation of being watched settled over me once more. I spun around in a circle but didn't see anyone. I peeked under my car and in the backseat before unlocking the door and slipping inside. With my heart pounding, I quickly locked the doors three times.

Five minutes went by with me breathing deeply to slow my heart rate. When my hands stopped shaking, I started the engine and pulled out of the parking lot. I was at a police station, for crying out loud. No one would be crazy enough to attack me there. I needed to stop letting my imagination take over my common sense.

Who was I kidding?

I wasn't going to be able to concentrate on work after everything that had already happened today. Besides, I promised Yanni I would meet him at his landscaping business about plants at some point this afternoon. Driving to the outskirts of town feeling the way I did made me uncomfortable. I realized my irrational fear was stupid, so I headed toward Yanni's Yards anyway. He was back from vacation with Claudett and said he had some new flowering bushes I wanted to plant now that the weather was warm enough.

I gave him a quick call and said I was on my way.

The rain started falling harder now, making it difficult to see. I turned my wipers on high and listened to the weather report on the radio. It didn't look like the rain would stop anytime soon. I was beginning to think it was a mistake to drive out to the country today.

Pulling over, I carefully turned my car around and started to drive back to town when a car headed in my direction turned their brights on, blinding me. I shielded my eyes and started to slow down when I realized the car had crossed the center line into my lane and was coming straight for me.

I screamed and jerked my steering wheel sharply to the right.

My car hydroplaned, spinning three-hundred-sixty degrees before rolling down an embankment. My Prius landed on its top with the engine hissing steam and the horn blaring. My head throbbed and I felt blood trickle down my temple. I hit the steering wheel with my fist, and the horn stopped, but a sound far more terrifying grew closer.

Footsteps on the pavement.

Someone was coming. I should be relieved but that wary sensation in my gut intensified. I had a horrible feeling whoever it was meant me harm. The footsteps grew muffled as they walked down the embankment. I couldn't see anything upside down. I couldn't even see their feet, so I had no idea if it was a man or a woman.

"Who's there?" I managed, but the pounding in my head was making me dizzy.

No answer.

"Please, help me," I croaked.

My car jerked and just as the door opened, the world went black around me.

18

My eyes fluttered open, and my head started pounding once more.

"Easy there, Kalli," Doc LaLone said. "You have a concussion."

"W-Where am I?" I blinked against the bright light.

"In the hospital. You were in a car accident and have been unconscious for the past twenty-four hours.

I searched my memory and suddenly the heart monitor beside my bed started beeping loudly as shadows crept back into my mind.

"Take it easy, Ballas. You've given me enough gray hairs," came a voice I'd know anywhere.

I looked past the doctor as he pushed some buttons on the machine to silence it. There was my handsome, disheveled detective looking exhausted and more than a little worried, hovering nearby.

Nik walked over to me and took my hand in his, lifting it to his mouth and kissing my fingers. "Please stop scaring the life out of me." *You're killing me, Ballas.*

"What happened?" I couldn't quite make out the foggy images in my brain.

"Your cousin, Yanni, called me when you didn't

show up at his landscaping business. He said you were on your way to pick out some new bushes for our yard. I got worried when the weather got worse, so I drove out there and saw your car off the side of the road. You hydroplaned."

"You're lucky Detective Stevens found you when he did," Doc LaLone said. "You have a pretty nasty gash on your head and were losing blood rather quickly."

"Who was there?" I looked at Nik.

"No one." He studied me curiously.

"Did you see tracks by my car?"

Nik frowned. "It was raining pretty hard. I'm sure it washed everything away. What kind of tracks?"

"Human tracks." I focused on my memories. "I remember now."

Nik's eyes widened. "Remember what?"

"After I left the police station, I was too distracted to work. So, I called Yanni. Now that he and Claudett are back from vacation, he asked me to come look at the flowering bushes we talked about buying. I figured that was as good a time as any, so I headed out. Halfway there, I realized the weather was getting worse, and I really shouldn't be driving out to the country alone. So, I pulled over and turned my car around."

"Wait, you turned around?" Nik's brow puckered.

My gaze met his and held as I nodded. "I had just started driving back to town when a car turned on its high beams, crossed the center line, and started driving right at me. I didn't hydroplane on my own, Nik."

"What are you saying?"

I inhaled a deep breath. "Someone forced me off the road on purpose."

Fear transformed his face and then anger hardened his features. "Did you get a good look at this guy, Kalli?"

"No, I have no idea if it was a man or a woman." My voice was shaky. "The last thing I remember is my car door opening seconds before I blacked out."

"There was no one around when I found you." He looked skeptical. "Maybe you were just delirious from losing so much blood."

"Maybe I imagined it, but it felt real." I looked at the doctor pleadingly. "Can I go home now?"

"I would prefer you stay another night, but I know how much you hate hospitals." Doc LaLone stared hard at me. "I will release you as long as you promise to take it easy, Kalli. A concussion is a big deal, and that gash on your head is full of stitches. Not to mention you're pretty banged up. I know you want to help clear your aunt's name but trust your boyfriend and let him do his job please."

Nik pointed at the doctor. "See? I'm not the only one who thinks you shouldn't be involved in this case. I hope you listen to him better than you listen to me."

"Cases, as in plural. And if you remember, it's not just my aunt's name I'm worried about. We own half of those puppies."

"Trust me, I haven't forgotten. Still, you need to have faith in me." His face softened. "Let me do my job and let me take care of you for once."

"Okay."

He arched one thick, black eyebrow high. "Okay?"

I nodded. "Take me home, Detective."

"You got it, Ballas."

It felt like it took forever for the release papers to come through, but I was finally home. My Prius was totaled, but honestly, I was a little afraid to drive after my ordeal. Wolfgang and Prissy were being especially attentive as I sat curled up on the couch with a blanket and a hot cup of tea. Nik hadn't let me lift a finger, and he hadn't left my side.

I adored him all the more for it.

"I love how sweet you're being, but one of us has to solve these cases." I looked at him over the top of my cup. "I will be fine. I have two great protectors here. So please ease my mind and get back to work."

"Are you sure?" He looked skeptical.

"I'm positive...but Detective?"

"Yeah?" Worry lines creased his face once more.

"I expect frequent updates." I smiled slowly.

He relaxed. "You got it, Ballas." He winked and then kissed my forehead before he rushed back to work.

I sat there for a long while when my doorbell suddenly rang. Wolf sprang to his feet and whined as he ran to the door. If I was in any danger, he would be growling not whining. That could only mean one thing.

My big fat Greek family was making a house call.

They'd gone to the hospital while I was unconscious, and then Nik had asked them to give me some space after I woke up and went home. This was their idea of space. I slowly unfolded my bruised and achy body from the couch and made my way to the locked door. Peering out the peephole, I couldn't help smiling as I let them in. My family might be crazy, but they were mine.

And I adored them.

"Oh, my baby!" Ma ran her hands all over me.

I winced. "Ouch. Careful. Ma, stop, please. I'm okay."

"Sit down. I put aloe on cut. And duct tape. Fix you

right up." She guided me back to the couch in the living room.

Aunt Tasoula carried in a crock of soup. Chloe carried in bread and salad. Leni followed her with dessert. Thalia joined them with a bouquet of flowers. And YiaYia Dido chased Frona who rode Wolfgang into the living room, holding his ears as reins, and singing, "Kalli Balli sat in her car, Kalli Balli spun very far, she bumped her head, we thought she was dead, cuz she couldn't get up in the morning."

"Ma, could you please get me my backpack?" I pointed by the door where Nik had left it. I needed pain medicine, but I wasn't about to tell Ma that. She would make me drink liquid aloe and put duct tape over where my body hurt for sure then.

"Of course, of course. My poor baby." Ma power walked over to the door, her polyester pants swishing with every step. She fetched my pack and brought it back to me. "There you have it. You rest. I cook. Okay? Okay." She joined the others in the kitchen.

I just sat still for a moment, until the pain became bearable, and then I opened my pack to find my pain reliever. Peeking inside as I rifled around, my hand suddenly stilled. With shaking fingers, I pulled out another note. It said...

I told you to back off. Now you see what "or else" can mean. You're lucky someone came along, or I would have finished you off on the side of the road. If you tell anyone about this note, next time, you won't be so lucky. Careful...I'm watching you.

I hadn't been delirious from loss of blood. One thing was becoming increasingly clear...someone wanted me dead and wouldn't stop until they succeeded.

~

A COUPLE DAYS LATER, I was feeling good enough to venture out of the house. I hadn't told Nik about the notes because I was afraid of what *or else* would entail if I did. I would just be on guard and keep practicing my self-defense moves.

I'd been working on my summer collection of designs and making good progress, but I had cabin fever. Even Ronald Banks wasn't there to keep me company. He was waiting for the last of the supplies to come in to finish our remodel so, in the meantime, he was doing work for other people until that happened.

I was bored and lonely.

I had promised Nik I wouldn't work any of the cases, but that didn't mean I couldn't get some fresh air. I decided to take Wolfgang for a walk. He needed the exercise, and I needed peace of mind knowing he would protect me from any danger. The sun was shining, birds were chirping, and a pleasant breeze was blowing.

What could possibly go wrong?

I strolled along our side street beneath the branches of the tree lined sidewalk, enjoying the day. I waved to neighbors and listened to children playing, laughing as I watched their antics. My smile faded. I knew I wanted to spend my life with Nik, but I still wasn't sure I wanted children.

The remodel was almost done, and we would officially be living together. That was a big step. It was only a matter of time before he might be contemplating an even bigger step, and he would have questions. Questions about what our future would look like.

Questions I wasn't prepared to answer.

I pulled my thoughts away from that and forced myself to tackle one thing at a time. Getting better. Staying safe. Clearing my aunt's name. Finding the missing puppies. I sighed. Why did life seem so complicated lately? Our cruise had been wonderful and relaxing. Maybe Clearview was the problem.

Maybe we needed another vacation.

I slowly shook my head. A vacation was only a Band-Aid. We still had real issues that needed to be resolved. All in good time. I focused on putting one foot in front of the other. The last thing I needed was to fall down and injure myself further. Nik would lock me up for my own good if that happened.

A straight jacket and mental ward didn't sound so bad at the moment.

I looked up. Someone was mowing their lawn. A little further down, I saw the mail truck. Winnie was delivering the mail, so I crossed the street to say hello. She rolled down the passenger side window as I approached.

"Hi, mate. You poor sheila. I heard what happened. Your cousins were worried sick. How's your noggin'?"

My cousins were almost as protective as my boyfriend. "Thanks. They're sweet." I gingerly touched the healing wound on my head. "It's getting better every day. How are you doing?"

"Kosmos didn't forget our six-month anniversary." She beamed. "He's taking me away for the weekend, the romantic bloke." She blushed. "He even gave me my present early. Thank you so much. I love them all."

"Oh, good, I'm so glad." I smiled wide, glad I

knocked them out the same day he okayed them. "Do you need any alterations?" Wolfgang jumped up on the side of the mail truck, and Winnie gave him a treat.

"Not a one." She rubbed the top of his massive head and then looked at me with gratitude. "You have an amazing eye. They fit perfectly."

"Great." I clapped, and Wolfgang whined. I patted him once then pointed to the ground and he sat without me so much as having to say a single command. "So, where is my romantic cousin taking you?"

"To a real live castle. Can you believe it?" Her voice vibrated with excitement. "I didn't know they even had those around here."

"Connecticut doesn't have any real medieval castles," I pointed out. "We have historic mansions and estates. But New York, especially the Hudson Valley region, has several castles that make great weekend getaways."

"I'm thrilled. Unlike France or Germany, Australia isn't that old of a country, so we don't have castles. I feel like a real live princess."

"You are a queen," I said with sincerity filling my voice. All women should be made to feel like queens by the men who love them. Nik sure did make me feel like one. "Sounds like my cousin made a good choice in an anniversary getaway place."

"He made a *great* choice." She winked. "Well, I best be on my way if I'm ever gonna finish my route."

"I won't keep you then. Say hi to Kos for me." I stepped out of the road and back to the sidewalk with Wolfgang by my side.

"Will do." She put her mail truck in drive and hit the gas pedal with her foot, the truck lurching forward in her haste.

"And I want to hear all about that castle when you get back," I hollered after her, thinking that might not be a bad choice for another getaway for Nik and me.

"You got it," she yelled back and then disappeared around the corner even faster than Aunt Tasoula.

Something told me she would have no trouble finishing her route on time.

Coming to the end of Picture Perfect Drive, I was about to turn back and go home, feeling a little tired. Wolfgang was having none of that. He ventured onto Main Street and pulled until I followed, my heart rate picking up pace.

For a moment, I looked around for kibble and women in black with nets.

Once my PTSD subsided, I followed along. I didn't exactly have another choice. He was stronger than I was. He sniffed the ground like he'd caught the scent of something, and he was on a mission. Out of curiosity, I let him have his way.

We passed all sorts of businesses, cafes, and restaurants. People window shopping, business owners sweeping out front of their shops and shining windows, men sitting outside of the barbershop playing checkers. Just an average day. Wolfgang didn't stop until we reached the end of Main Street, all the way to Dino's Daycare.

"Ahhh, so that's why you were on a mission. You miss your friends, don't you." Nik had insisted he not go to daycare to play because he wanted him home to babysit me.

Wolfgang whined and wagged his tail.

"Okay, buddy, how about I take you inside to play for just a little while. It'll be our little secret. I won't tell Daddy if you don't? Deal?" I held out my hand.

Wolf lifted his paw into my palm, and we shook.

We walked through the front door, but I didn't see Dino or Milly. A young teenager was working at the front desk.

When he looked up, I smiled. "Hey, Christos, I didn't know you worked here?"

Christos was Aunt Tasoula's grandson. He started out working in her salon, sweeping up the floor before he was old enough to get a job anywhere else. His pop, Adonis, was her only son, and according to Aunt Tasoula, Adonis's wife was lazy and useless. My cousin was thirty-eight and Christos was sixteen.

"Hey, Kalli." He smiled. "Mr. Willis finally hired me to help out Milly. It sure beats sweeping up Yia-Yia's salon."

"Just like my job sure beats washing dishes at Ma's restaurant," I pointed out.

He laughed. "My YiaYia's crazy."

"Can I let you in on a little secret?" I leaned forward. "So's my ma."

We both laughed at that.

"Is Wolfy here to play?" he asked.

"Yes, but don't tell Detective Stevens. He thinks I need a babysitter."

"I feel you. So does my pop think I do." Christos rolled his eyes, and I wondered if that was how I looked.

"Okay, well, I will be back in a few hours." I handed him Wolfgang's leash.

The dog just sat there, stubbornly, and whined.

"You sure he wants to play?" Christos arched a brow, looking remarkably like Aunt Tasoula.

"He dragged me all the way here. I'm sure he'll be fine once he gets back there." I patted Wolf on the head and told him to go.

He still just sat there.

Christos shrugged. "Maybe it's separation anxiety. I read about that before starting work here. He'll probably be fine once you're gone."

"Hmmm, he's never been like that before. Maybe it's because I am injured. He's very protective. I'll go, but if he gives you any problems, call my cell."

"I will." Christos tugged on the leash.

I walked out the door and stood in the parking lot, not quite sure what to do with myself. It was so strange not having a car. Maybe I would kill a few hours in a café and then go back for him. I started to head for the sidewalk, when I felt someone walking up behind me. My heart started pounding. Balling my fists and positioning my stance, I whirled around, ready to take on my attacker.

Milly Donovan-Rockwell stopped short and blinked at me, startled.

"Sorry," I said, and lowered my hands. "Call it a reflex."

"No, I'm the sorry one for sneaking up on you. But once I saw you, I knew it was time I told you the truth."

"The truth?" I blinked. "About what?"

"Actually, let me show you instead." She took my hand and pulled me after her. *A Picture's worth a thousand words, and no one's going to believe me unless I prove it. I need you to come with me. I won't take no for an answer. Strength in numbers. I need that to have the courage for what I'm about to do.*

"Milly, what's going on? What do you need courage for?"

She dropped my hand and took a step back, eying me warily. "H-How did you know I was thinking that?"

"Your thoughts are written all over your face," I lied.

She blew out a breath. "Oh, I guess they probably are. Just please come with us."

"Us?" My eyes widened.

She pointed to the mysterious woman I had seen her get into the car with outside of Full Disclosure a while back. "Yes, us. We were just about to leave, and I think this is something you're going to want to be around for."

I followed her over to the woman and into the big white van, wondering what in Mount Olympus I had gotten myself into.

19

Riding in the back of a white unmarked van gave me serial killer vibes. Who was this woman Milly brought me to? I kept my eyes trained on my surroundings so I could find my way back if I was being abducted. I'd asked Milly a couple more times where we were going and who this woman was, but she insisted on showing me.

Nik was going to be so mad at me.

I couldn't think about that now. There had been something in Milly's voice that propelled me to go with her. We traveled towards the outskirts of town in the same direction as my cousin's landscaping business. It wasn't raining today. Still, I had to breathe deeply not to be traumatized from my previous crash.

It wasn't long before we crossed the town line and stopped down the road from an old, abandoned farmhouse, then parked behind a group of trees out of sight.

"Where are we?" I asked as we got out of the van.

"I'll explain later. My friend, Lara, here has been staking this place out." She pointed to the woman. "There shouldn't be anyone here at this time of day, so this a good time to strike." Milly motioned for me to follow her. She handed me some nets while she grabbed what looked like a catch pole.

"Strike?" I gasped. "Maybe I should call Detective Stevens."

"When the opportunity presented itself, we had to leave immediately, but I'll notified the proper authorities if our suspicions are correct." Lara carried a tranquilizer gun.

"Which are…?" I raised a brow as I shifted the nets in my arms.

"Later." Lara held up her finger in a shushing gesture as we neared the house.

I had a bad feeling about this.

The driveway was empty. Looking around one last time, Lara led the way to the back of the house. She tried the door, but it was locked. So, she found a nearby rock and broke the window above the doorknob. Carefully reaching inside, she unlocked the door and opened it. We were breaking and entering?

It was definitely a full moon.

I'd come this far, and I was already guilty by association, so I might as well finish the journey. I needed to see what was so important on the other side of this door. We entered the house, but it looked like no one had lived here for decades. Milly and I silently followed Lara upstairs, downstairs, and into the basement.

Whatever she was looking for wasn't there.

We headed back outside. "I can't believe we were wrong." Milly's shoulders slumped. "I was so positive I was right."

"About what?" I asked, tired of being out of the loop.

Milly opened her mouth to speak but Lara cut her off.

"Hang on." Lara pointed out back by the barn. "You still might be."

We hurried after her. The barn was filled with old equipment and rusted tools, but that was about it. A stray cat shrieked and ran out of a hole in the back. We all jumped.

"Okay, I'm out." I turned in the other direction, intending to leave, but then I stopped. "What's this?" I pointed to a door in the floor.

"Great idea," Milly said eagerly.

"That's an old root cellar," Lara pointed out. "They were used back in the day as cold storage for fruits and vegetables before refrigeration. Today some people still use them to store food as well as a storm shelter or safe room." She looked at Milly. "You ready with that catch pole?"

Milly nodded and held the pole in front of her with two hands.

Lara readied her tranquilizer gun and looked at me. "Be ready with the nets."

"Okay, I guess." I opened the nets and held them in front of me for Zeus only knew what.

Lara leaned down and grabbed the door then flung it open. She quickly led the way into the root cellar with Milly and me hot on her heels. I heard what they were looking for long before I saw them.

Twenty-two yipping Saint Berdoodle puppies and two very loud adult dogs barking.

I started shaking with relief, and tears filled my eyes as the dogs came into view. They looked wonderful, like they'd been taken very good care of. When lost or neglected dogs were found, they were often in survival mode. Scared and afraid animals could behave aggressively and must learn to trust all over again.

It was clear these dogs had not been abused. They had plush dog beds, food, water, toys, and a clean pen. Someone knew what they were doing. In a pen right next to them, were the Coopers' purebred show dog golden retrievers. They were in equally great shape.

"Who are you?" I asked Lara.

"I've been friends with Milly for years. I'm an animal control officer for the town of Lakeshore." She set her tranquilizer gun down, knowing we didn't need it for these animals.

"Don't you officers wear marked uniforms and drive marked vehicles?" I eyed her suspiciously.

"We normally don't go undercover, but Milly insisted we needed the element of surprise to pull this off."

"Why all the secrecy?" I asked Milly.

"So that—"

Before she could answer, we heard a noise behind us. Whirling around, I was shocked to see Hannah Schwartz and Blair Kingsley tied up with duct tape over their mouths. Milly gasped, and I raced over to the women and carefully peeled off their duct tape, while Lara pulled out her phone to call the proper authorities.

Too late.

The sound of a hammer being pulled back on a gun made us all freeze.

"I wouldn't do that if I were you," came a woman's voice.

We slowly turned around, and there stood Raven Monroe pointing a gun at us.

"Tie them up by the others," she said to the man beside her.

Dino Willis looked at Milly with regret and sorrow

in his eyes, but that didn't stop him from doing what he was told.

"How could you, Dino?" Milly asked quietly. "This isn't the man I know."

"She made me do it," he said, pointing to his still bruised eye. "I didn't want to do any of it, but I didn't have a choice. I was in too deep."

"You're weak," Raven spat, looking at him with disgust. "If you had paid me what you owed me, none of this would have happened."

"I tried to warn you about her," Hannah chimed in, "but you wouldn't listen to me. I dated a man once when I was on a standup comedy tour who used her as his booking agent, only she is involved in illegal off-track betting. Trust me when I say she is ruthless if she doesn't get what she wants."

"That's right, and he has the black eye to prove it," Raven said. "Stealing the dogs and selling them to pay me back was Dino's idea. Kidnapping you to shut you up was mine, and I enjoyed every minute of it. Look who has the last laugh now. I should have finished you off with that sedative when I had the chance." She leveled the gun. "You shouldn't have stuck your nose in where it didn't belong."

"Why kidnap *me*?" Blair asked. "What did I ever do to you?"

"Your husband's loaded, princess," Raven replied. "I decided I'd earned a bonus after all the crap Dino has put me through. I had planned on letting you go after I was paid a hefty ransom and was long gone." She looked at Lara, Milly, and me. "But now after your meddling friends got involved to save the day, I can't leave any loose ends behind."

"Look, I might have a gambling problem and have stolen some puppies, but I never agreed to kidnapping people, and I'm definitely not a killer." Dino held up his hands and backed away towards the entrance.

"You're not going anywhere, darling." Raven turned the gun on him. "Like I said, you're weak. Did you really think I planned to leave you alive? Get over with the women and tie yourself to Milly since you're so fond of her."

Dino's mouth fell open, but he did as she requested, muttering, "You're a monster."

"You have no idea," she sneered.

Once they were all tied up, Raven slipped her gun in her back pocket and fished Lara's keys to her van out of her pocket. "Thanks for the ride, *officer*." She laughed. "I was wondering how I was going to transport twenty-two puppies and two full-sized dogs, plus the bonus goldens, to the buyers I have lined up."

"You won't get away with this," Lara said.

"Oh, I think I just did." Raven winked.

"I told Detective Stevens about your threatening notes," I lied. "He gave me a tracker. He'll be here in minutes."

Raven hesitated. "You're lying. I didn't leave any threatening notes."

"Oh, I think you're the one who's lying."

She stared at me for a long minute then went over to my backpack and started digging through it. "There's no tracker in here."

"Who said the tracker was a *thing*?" I looked behind her.

She whirled around, but it was too late. Wolfgang lunged at her and flattened her on her back, pinning her to the ground. I'd heard him before he'd come down the stairs to find us. I'd know that snorting, sniffing, snotty snout anywhere...

And I'd never loved him more.

"Wolf, stay," I said and then blinked. "Priscilla?" Now, *that* I hadn't seen coming. Where on earth had she come from?

My prissy calico cat trotted regally over to me and started chewing at the rope around my wrists. Finally, the rope broke free. I would untie the others in a minute. First, I needed to keep us safe. Wolf was stubborn, but he listened to me. Still, even I didn't know how long he would hold a stay. I scrambled over and grabbed Raven's gun from the floor just as Wolf decided to say hello to his girlfriends, Chanel and Versace.

Raven rolled to her feet.

"Don't move another inch." I prayed she wouldn't call my bluff.

She took a step toward me. "You don't know how to use a gun."

"No, but I do, so I suggest you listen to the lady," came a male voice that was music to my ears.

Raven sneered but wisely did as she was told.

I spun around with shaking hands and carefully handed the gun to Nik. *You did great, Ballas.* He winked and took the gun from me with one hand and slipped it into the back of his jeans while keeping his own gun trained on Raven the whole time. He tossed me the handcuffs, and I gladly handcuffed her while he called his backup in.

"How did you find us? And how are our pets here?" I hugged him as a swarm of officers came in to arrest Raven and Dino, untie the women, and rescue the dogs.

"Let's just say it was a family affair." He kissed the top of my head before letting me go. "Christos called me. He said he called you, but you didn't answer your phone."

"Oh, whoops, I left it in the van by mistake."

"Well, he called me to let me know that Wolf escaped from daycare." Nik raised a brow at me. "Imagine my surprise since we agreed he would stay with you."

"I can explain."

"I'm listening."

"Wolf really wanted to go for a walk, and he acted like he had picked up a scent. He was insistent on leading me to Dino's Daycare. I thought he just wanted to play. So, I let him. Then I ran into Milly and Lara outside, and they really wanted to show me something. My gut told me to go, so I did. I was going to call you, but they said not yet. Then, when we found the dogs and the women, it was too late. Raven and Dino found us." I studied him. "So now that you know my story, what's yours? How did *you* find us?"

"When Wolf escaped, the tracker in his collar is linked to your phone so I couldn't track him. I went home to see if he was there and found both he and Prissy alone and unsettled. I knew something was wrong. I also called you, but you didn't answer. Thank the gods you share your location with me, so I was able to track you. The animals insisted on coming with me. As soon as I saw the van and opened the door, they jumped out and took off. Call it animal instinct, or maybe when they got loose before, they tracked the puppies here before getting lost in the woods in the storm. Whatever the reason, I'm just grateful to have found you and the kidnapped women and the puppies. You just solved most of our cases in one day. But Ballas...?"

"Yes, Detective?"

"Please don't do that again."

"Okay." I stood on my toes and kissed him. *I*

couldn't handle it if anything ever happened to you. "Ditto," I whispered.

The crisis team escorted Hannah and Blair outside to a waiting ambulance to be checked over by EMTs and questioned by Lakeshore police officers. Nolan was already on the scene with his camera and microphone in hand. Even though this case ended in Lakeshore, it originated in Clearview, so Captain Crenshaw was on the scene as well.

Nik and I had walked out with Milly and Lara to join the animal control team who was loading the puppies and dogs into the van to have them checked out by the vet back in Clearview since the animals weren't strays. They belonged to Boomer and Jaz. Boomer rode with them and was on the phone with Jaz.

I could hear her crying through the phone line before he got into the vehicle.

I held Prissy, and Nik had attached Wolf's leash to his collar then took Prissy from me and walked over to put them both in his car. I crossed my arms over my chest and watched as Clearview police officers walked past us with Raven and Dino in handcuffs. There was no way Nik would let them go to the Lakeshore jail.

"One thing I don't understand," I said to Raven before they could help her into the squad car.

She scowled at me. "And here I thought you had all the answers? Guess you're not as smart as you think you are."

I ignored the jab, determined to get to the truth. "How was Skylar Delaney a loose end in your puppy-napping and kidnapping scheme?"

She snorted. "Look, I don't even know who that is."

"The woman you murdered in my aunt's salon, Hera's Halo."

"You're crazy, lady. I didn't murder anyone. I just wanted money. You should know all about bluffing, Annie Oakley." She let the officers fold her into the squad car and left me with more questions than answers.

Who sent me those threatening notes...and did we still have a killer on the loose?

20

Sunday brunch we were all at Ma's and Pop's, counting our blessings.

Wolfgang, Chanel, Versace, and all twenty-two Saint Berdoodles were running around the yard. Frona was in her glory, bouncing and playing and socializing with the puppies. YiaYia looked especially exhausted. Frona had finally met her match in energy. None of the dogs acted as if they had a care in the world. There didn't seem to be any aftereffects from their ordeal. Dino might be a lot of things, but he loved animals and had taken good care of them.

Still...

We were all on the same page of not wanting to let any of them out of our sights. I got a lump in my throat watching the runt try to keep up with the rest of the litter. It was apparently a maternal thing because Ma hadn't taken her eyes off me since I'd gotten home from my standoff with a sociopathic, gun toting, kidnapper, dog-napper, potential killer.

"Sit. I cook. You eat." Ma pushed me down onto a chair then shoved a plate in my lap. "You pale. I get more aloe."

"Ma, I'm fine. I don't..." It fell on deaf ears, so I

gave up trying to argue with a Greek mama. It was pointless.

"You too skinny to make Greek babies." Pop handed me a second plate and a roll of duct tape. "Here. Put this on you head. It draw the concussion right out through you pores. There you have it."

I glanced over at Nik, but he was deep in conversation with Captain Crenshaw and hadn't heard, thank you Zeus. I looked back at my pop. "I'm pretty sure that's not how it works, Pop." I took the plate and tape after seeing the silent, stubborn determination in his eyes. "But thank you." I smiled overly brightly and showed all my teeth until he finally walked away.

Leni had actually brought Clint to brunch and was holding his hand. The mamas were so pleased. Nolan had left town since he'd gotten what he came for, aka the gossip on the Kingsleys, and it was clear Leni had chosen Clint. He was a better fit anyway, since he lived in Clearview already and looked Greek enough.

That left Jasper and Vicky. She didn't come today, saying she felt ill. It was hard to tell if they only had a friend vibe between them. I'd never seen them acting romantically towards each other no matter how hard Ma tried to make it so. He sat at a table with my other cousins, looking completely content by himself. Thalia and the senator sat at a table with Jaz and Boomer, most likely talking about the closing on their new house.

Aunt Tasoula walked in late, making a grand entrance in her most dazzling evening gown yet. She had her arm regally looped through a smiling Tate's, who wore a tuxedo and carried her final baton. Everyone clapped, and my aunt took a bow, then made her way over to me.

Let the circus begin.

"And how my favorite niece?" I was her only niece. She kissed my cheek. *Greek men like curves. Great idea for lingerie. Padded undies. Maybe I—*

"Okay, then." I pulled away.

"Okay what?" Her brow would be puckered if she hadn't had so much Botox.

"I mean I'm okay." I touched my head. The stitches were out. I still got headaches but not nearly as bad.

"Ah, that good." She placed the back of her hand on her forehead. "Oh, woe is me, we worry so."

Tate immediately steadied her. "You okay, my love?"

She sighed dramatically. "I okay now. You good man. My throat parched. Hint hint."

"H2O?" he asked.

"OUZO." She fluttered her fake eyelashes at him.

He grinned wider then hurried off to fetch her a drink.

I tried not to roll my eyes. "Now you know how we feel when you worry us."

"Bah." She waved her hand at me. "Killer caught. No worry."

"If you say so." I shrugged.

"I do." She frowned. "I say so. That what I say." She glanced at the wound on my head once more. "You sure you okay? You a little confused."

I closed my eyes for a moment and changed the subject. "So, I see the Majorette has come to an end, and you picked a winner?"

Her face lit up and she clapped her hands. "Ah, yes. The finale. My Viking always the one. He just need reminiscing."

"And now I supposed you're in after-the-final-baton-happily-ever-after bliss." I smiled and meant it. "I'm happy for you, Aunt Tasoula."

"You have good man too." She looked at Nik. "Maybe he need baton too."

"I'll keep that in mind." My gaze followed hers over to my dreamy detective, and he was staring at me. The butterflies danced in my stomach as they always did when he looked at me. He smiled as if he read my mind, and I blushed.

"Oh, my Hercules." Aunt Tasoula jumped.

"What's wrong?" I frowned.

"The buzzer go off."

I was a little afraid to ask exactly what buzzer she might be referring to.

She pulled her cell phone out of her bra pocket and waved it at Nik as she shuffled over there in her tight dress and high heels with me right behind her. "Yoo hoo, the thingy go beep, beep, beep. How I make it stop?"

Nik looked at her phone and then at me and finally at my aunt. "The silent alarm I had installed in the back room of Hera's Halo just went off."

~

EVERYTHING HAPPENED AT ONCE.

The silent alarm was a backup alarm that only went off if the real alarm was disabled. Nik had told us to stay put while he and Boomer went to investigate what had triggered the silent alarm. Of course, Aunt Tasoula wouldn't listen. She said she had a headache and was going home to wait for news.

I said I was tired, but Jaz was still busy talking to Thalia. Everyone else was still brunching. Jaz offered to drop my pets home later so they could still play, and I asked my aunt if she would mind giving me a ride home since I still didn't have a car and wasn't supposed to drive with my concussion. She agreed, and we slipped out before Ma found out people had left her brunch early.

As soon as we got in the car, I turned to my aunt. "Look, we both know you have no intention of going home."

"My salon my baby. I need to see myself she okay."

"I get it, but I'm coming with you. Nik and Boomer are there. We will wait outside until they give us the *all clear*."

"Okay. We do your way." She put the car in drive and peeled away from the curb before I even had my seatbelt buckled. Pumping her fist in the air, she yelled, "Let's ride!"

I suddenly feared riding with my aunt was the most dangerous thing of all.

Aunt Tasoula got a look in her eyes that I recognized all too well, and it spelled trouble.

"What are you doing?" I squeaked.

"I saw in movie once. You no let them see you coming. We park next door. No righty flighty. We go lefty loogie!" She missed the driveway, jumped the curb, bounced the tires twice, yanked the wheel to the left, and finally we skidded to a stop in the neighboring building's front yard after spinning like a top.

My heart jumped in my throat, and it took several minutes to regulate my breathing and get the dizziness to stop. "Are you crazy?" I finally got out.

"No, I good." She winked and then opened her door and got out.

"Hey, I thought we were waiting for the *all clear*." I ran to catch up with her.

She looked up at the sky and shrugged. "Look clear to me." My aunt marched right up to the front door of her salon and used her key to let herself in before I could stop her.

I didn't see Nik and Boomer, so I hurried in after her. "This is a bad idea."

We heard voices coming from the back room.

"It has to be in here somewhere. We must have missed something, no?" said a male voice with an unmistakable French accent.

Antoine Dupont.

My aunt's lips parted, and she started marching forward, but this time, I grabbed her arm and whispered, "Wait. This is our chance to see what they're up to."

We peeked through the crack in the door. Antione and Louis were dressed all in black. They had torn the room apart, looking for something. Antoine sat on Hera's throne, running a hand over his slicked back hair as he looked around the room.

"If Benjamin Delaney wasn't already dead, I would kill him myself," Louis spat. "No one steals from us and gets away with it."

"Do you think Skylar knew what her husband was up to?" Antione slid off the throne and dropped to the floor, ripping up yet another floorboard.

"I don't think she knew the money was counterfeit, or she wouldn't have been spending it all over town." Louis kept sliding his hands along the wall as if searching for a secret room. "Ben knew better than that."

"Maybe she found it before he left and didn't tell him. Or he forgot some, and then after he died, she found it. Either way, the money wasn't hers. It's ours."

"It's no one's because it's not real." Vicky walked into the room from a back exit and held a gun on them. "Special Agent Victoria Nettles." She flashed her badge and tossed a pair of handcuffs to them. "Handcuff yourselves together now."

Antoine and Louis did as she asked, and she holstered her weapon.

Aunt Tasoula ran into the room. "Oh, thank Hera you feeling better, Vicky."

I scrambled after her. "I don't think she was ever sick, Aunt Tasoula."

"I've been after the Dupont brothers for years. Ben Delaney was in the international trade business, buying and selling goods and services between countries. The brothers offered their counterfeit services to him as well as people from other countries. They are the head of the counterfeit currency ring for several countries." Vicky moved to the side. "Come on in, Detectives."

Nik and Boomer came through the back entrance and stopped short when they saw Aunt Tasoula and me.

"Whose idea was this?" Nik asked.

Aunt Tasoula and I pointed at each other simultaneously.

"We ran into Special Agent Nettles out back, exchanged credentials, and then prepared things for her to make the arrest." Boomer looked between the two of us. "How did you two even get here?"

Aunt Tasoula said, "I plead five."

"What she said." I nodded toward my aunt.

Nik narrowed his eyes at me, waiting.

I sighed. "I'll tell you later. It's a long story." I looked at Vicky. "What I want to know is how did the Dupont brothers even know to come to Clearview?"

"Ben ripped them off and fled the United States, but his plane went down over the ocean," Vicky went on. "Skylar must have found some of the bills and started spending it in Clearview. When the story hit the news, it drew the brothers to Clearview. Skylar didn't know who they were or their connection to her late husband, but they knew who she was. So, they wooed her, but when she wouldn't give them the money, they killed her."

"We're thieves, not killers," Antoine said.

"We figured whoever did kill her must have been chasing her the night of Prom," Louis added. "She was with us, but something startled her, and she ran off. We figured she must have hidden the rest of the money in the back of this salon, but it's not here. We've looked everywhere."

"Not everywhere," Aunt Tasoula said smugly. She walked over to Hera's throne and turned her crown. A trapped door popped open in the bottom. She reached down and looked. "Just as I thought." She pulled out a duffel bag full of money. "Skylar and I have big fight. She come in back room and touch my things. We scuffle, and she grab Hera's crown to stop from falling. Pop go the Willie. Trap door open. She must have remembered that and hid money there."

"I'll take that." Vicky reached for the bag.

"No, I'll take that." Clayton walked into the room, the only one now holding a gun.

Nik, Boomer, and Vicky all held their hands ready and hovering over their weapons.

"Don't even think about it," Clayton said. "I'll shoot the women before any of you can get a shot off at me."

"Clayton, you no shoot me. I the Majorette." Aunt Tasoula took a step toward him.

"Try me, Tasoula," he ground out. "You've been trying my patience for weeks with those stupid batons."

"You just upset cuz you bald." Aunt Tasoula nodded at him with pity.

"For the last time, I'm not bald." He yanked the black wig off his head and ripped off the fake mustache, then swiped contacts out of his eyes. "See?"

My aunt gaped at him. "You a blue-eyed silver fox. Why hide that?"

"Ben Delaney?" Antoine sputtered.

"You're alive?" Louis added in disbelief.

"And kickin'," Ben growled. "I'm an expert pilot. I knew how to parachute out and fake my own death. Everything would have been perfect if I hadn't missed a bag. I was broke, but I had life insurance. Skylar would have been set, and so would I, in another country. But when the counterfeit story hit the news, I had to come back to stop the bills from circulating or the rest would be no good."

"Poor Skylar," my aunt said in disbelief.

"Have you met my wife?" Ben said, then sighed. "She was difficult at best, but I didn't want to kill her. I had no choice. She saw past my disguise and threatened to expose me. She wouldn't tell me where she hid the money. She started calling Tate, so I had to shut her up. Framing you was a necessity."

"You no worthy of my baton." Aunt Tasoula thrust her chin up high.

"No, he's not." I hugged her.

"You no silver fox." My aunt looked at him with disgust. "You a silver snake."

"And you're a—"

Suddenly, he was tackled to the floor by a flash of polyester and black hair, and the gun went flying from his hand.

"You no talk to my sister like that. She a Greek mama, and you no gentleman." Ma knelt on his back, and everyone just stared at her. "Well, no just stand there! Let's go, boys. My knees no good no more. I old you know." She held out her hand.

Vicky rushed to help her up.

Nik scrambled over to cuff Ben.

Boomer helped the brothers to their feet.

Aunt Tasoula and I stared dumbstruck.

"Let's take a ride, gentlemen," Boomer said.

"We'll take them to the station for processing, then you can transfer them when everything's ready," Nik said to Vicky.

"Thank you, Detectives." Vicky nodded once as they left, adding, "I'll meet you there in a few minutes."

"You have a gun?" Ma looked at Vicky then felt her forehead. "You no sick." She looked at Aunt Tasoula. "Clayton have silver hair? The Frenchies dress like black bulldogs. Why you car in the neighbor's lawn? And you," she pointed at me, "why you no home resting? No one leave my Sunday brunch early." She made the sign of the cross and then crossed her arms over her ample bosom. "Someone wanna tell me what go on here before my muffins get cold?"

EPILOGUE

az and Boomer closed on their new house and were preparing for their wedding, while the remodel on the house Nik and I rented was finally finished. We'd settled on a very small water fountain to appease both our families. Yanni had tucked it tastefully among the landscaping of colored rocks and flowering bushes Nik and I had finally ordered. Jaz offered to sell the house to us, but we decided moving in together was enough for now.

Nik and I sat in our new great room on a big corner couch in front of the fireplace with the news streaming on the TV above it. Blair was in the hospital with Grant catering to her every want or need and the nanny taking care of the children.

"The Kingsleys appear to be reconciling." Nik took a sip of his steaming hot black coffee.

"Something tells me he will be paying for his indiscretions for years to come." I blew on my hot tea. "Speaking of indiscretions, Jack Harris has been kicked off the school board and publicly disgraced. His wife left him and is moving to Florida with her sister. Not sure what he plans to do, but I doubt he'll be commissioning any more lingerie from me any time soon."

"I heard he was already on the dating apps. It doesn't surprise me." Nik shook his head. "Did I tell you we finally found Chelsea Turner?" He crossed his ankles on the coffee table in front of the couch over top of a curled-up Wolfgang who was snoring lightly on the floor beneath his legs.

"No. I was wondering what happened to her?" I curled my legs up beneath me, trying not to disturb a sleeping Prissy on the cushion beside me, breathing like a respectable lady...she wouldn't dream of snoring.

"Well, apparently Chelsea was located on an island in the South Pacific. Turns out she played a scratch off while getting gas after she checked out of Lakeshore Heights, and she won big. She figured her name was cleared with Grant as her alibi, and it was a sign she was meant to move on. So, she left, retired from being a flight attendant, and is now living with a man half her age and loving every minute of it."

"Wow, good for her." I laughed. "Ma said Drake Fontanna is staying in town. She's not too happy about that. Says he really is a traitor. I guess he is teaming up with Vincenzo Ricci as his partner, and they're renaming the restaurant Vincenzo Fontanna's Italian restaurant. Vinny probably figures two Italians will finally beat one Greek, but he should know better. Ma isn't playing that game. She upped his ante with turning one Greek restaurant into two by working with Thalia to buy a building and open a second restaurant soon."

"Thalia mentioned that to my ma." Nik chuckled. "Vinny should have known one Greek *anything* meant an entire Greek family. And there you have it."

We both laughed.

"Ma also told me Ursula and her fiancé Tammy left town just as quickly as they could. Apparently, she'd forgotten what small-town living was like and remembered why she left in the first place. She's ready to get back to the big city and the courtroom she loves. She gave Aunt Tasoula free rein to plan as many reunions as she wants. The only party Ursula want to plan is her wedding."

"I'm sure your aunt loves that." Nik took another sip of his coffee. "By the way, Helen was thrilled to see her sister Hannah home safe and sound. She tried to talk her into sticking around, but Hannah was itching to get back on tour and back on the road."

"I don't blame her." I nodded. "It's clear Tate has eyes for only one woman. The majorette who gave him her last baton." I sighed dreamily and then giggled.

"Your aunt and her crazy shenanigans." Nik chuckled, his eyes locking onto mine and his electric blue gaze holding mine captive. "There's something about those Ballas women."

"And those charming Stevens men." I smiled tenderly. "Speaking of captivating couples, whatever happened to Malik and Keisha Cooper?"

"They took their dogs and their camper and headed home, forgoing the rest of the season's dog shows. They said this whole ordeal made them realize just how important family is." Nik's eyes filled with a longing I couldn't ignore. "They were anxious to get back to their children and grandchildren. Can't say that I blame them."

I looked away first and cleared my throat, admitting, "There is something special about having a family." That was as much as I was ready to admit at the moment. Just saying the words made my heart race.

He seemed to read my mind and let the matter drop. "Special Agent Nettles has moved on to her next assignment. She got a promotion after bringing in the Dupont brothers and the resurrected Ben Delaney."

"I still can't believe Clayton was really Skylar's late husband, and that he faked his own death. That's like something you see in the movies. I'm even more surprised that Vicky was FBI. She was such a good handywoman."

"You and me both."

"Ma is still recovering from her failed attempt at matchmaking, but something tells me Jasper will be just fine."

Nik laughed. "I'm sure you're right. As for Raven and Dino, they will both do time in jail. Raven has outstanding warrants in several counties. Dino will do time for a lesser sentence followed by getting the help he needs for his gambling addiction. Thank the gods that Milly overheard a couple of their conversations and suspected they were the ones who had taken the puppies. If she hadn't known that his late grandmother had left him the ancient family farm, she never would have known where to look."

"I can't believe he was in so much debt and none of us knew. I heard the bank repossessed the daycare, and Milly was able to buy it and just in time. She gave Christos a raise, and then gave birth to a beautiful baby girl. I'm so happy for her and Nelson. They're great parents already." I smiled, thinking they made the perfect little family. Maybe having a baby wouldn't be so scary after all. Then my smile slipped. "Speaking of babies, I can't believe I'm actually going to miss all those puppies. I just hope they're happy in their new homes."

All the twenty-two Saint Berdoodle puppies got adopted, which was bittersweet.

"I have a feeling they will be," Nik said with a twinkle in his eye.

"What is that look for, Detective?" I was never one who liked surprises. It meant I wasn't in control, and not being in control was a scary thing for me.

"Hold that thought, Ballas." My handsome detective jogged off into one of the guest bedrooms, and then returned with a puppy I recognized immediately. The runt of the litter. He carefully set the tiny black, brown, and white Saint Berdoodle in my lap and said, "Meet Willow."

I took one look into her weepy big brown eyes and fell madly in love all over again. Prissy was mine, and Wolfgang was his, but Willow was ours. The start of our own little family, and I suddenly realized my heart didn't race one single bit.

BOOKS BY KARI LEE TOWNSEND

KALLI BALLAS MYSTERY

Mind Over Murder

Two Cents of Doom

A Touch of Malice

An Inkling of Evil

Mayhem on the Mind

CECE MONROE MYSTERY

Harmful Habits

SUNNY MEADOWS MYSTERY

Tempest in the Tea Leaves

Corpse in the Crystal Ball

Trouble in the Tarot

Shenanigans in the Shadows

Perish in the Palm

Hazard in the Horoscope

Chaos and Cold Feet

Murder in the Meditation

DIGITAL DIVA

Talk to the Hand

Rise of the Phenoteens

BOOKS BY KARI LEE HARMON

COLDWATER COVE

Dark Seas

Frozen Waters

Dangerous Thaw

Deadly Frost

STANDALONE NOVELS

Valley of Secrets

Until Tomorrow

Project Produce

Love Lessons

LAKEHOUSE TREASURES NOVELLAS

James

Amber

Meghan

Brook

MERRY SCROOG-MAS NOVELLAS

Naughty or Nice

Sleigh Bells Ring

Jingle all the Way

TRIPLE R RANCH SHORT STORIES

Destiny Wears Spurs

Spurred by Fate

ABOUT THE AUTHOR

Kari Lee Townsend is a National Bestselling Author of mysteries & a tween superhero series. She also writes romance and women's fiction as Kari Lee Harmon. With a background in English education, she's now a full-time writer, wife to her own superhero, mom of 3 sons, 1 darling diva, 1 daughter-in-law & 2 lovable fur babies. These days you'll find her walking her dogs or hard at work on her next story, living a blessed life.